HANNAH
& THE GODS OF
OLYMPUS

Written By Charles Eagen Lord

Cover Art By Luis Lasahido

Maiden Comics Studios, Copyright 2014

All Rights Reserved

Maiden Comics Studios
Charlotte, NC 28241 USA
www.facebook.com/godsofolympusbooks
www.theGodsofOlympus.com
www.MaidenComics.com

Published by Maiden Comics Studios, 2014

ISBN-10: 0-692-25620-2
ISBN-13: 978-0-692-25620-6

Published in the United States of America
Author: Charles Eagen Lord

"Dangerous, therefore, is it to take shelter under a tree, during a thunder-gust. It has been fatal to many, both men and beasts."

- Benjamin Franklin

I. MIDSUMMER

Hannah swam all summer, mornings mostly, when she knew the pool at Prep would be empty. Her father assumed she'd swim for the team again, but Hannah was not herself sure. The water though, cool and quiet to her, was one of the few places Hannah could go to clear her head of all that had gone so wrong.

She never used a clock those mornings, judging her time instead by feel. Hers, Hannah felt, was not fast enough. Still, she swam lap after lap, the water's embrace reward enough, solitude enough those mornings of that summer that seemed to pass so slow.

Hannah wondered how disappointed her father would be if she chose not to compete, deciding though that she would never know. If she quit the team, he'd be fine with it and not say a word to her. It was the same with her grades. Hannah had kept them up, but studying, she would wonder what her father would say if she brought home a failing mark. Maybe in the fall she would find out, if she even lasted that long.

Hannah wondered too how disappointed her father would be to learn of everything- that she grieved her mother's passing as intensely as ever, more so then since when she'd first passed, that she kept from her father so much, to save his face more than hers, that she felt crushed by the town they lived in, her father's enormous presence in it the weight at times heaviest of all on her, and wondered greatest how her father might feel about the very deep despair she'd suffered since Spring. His disappointment would be nothing next to the grief she'd have caused him. Hadn't he had enough, or would Hannah be, as she feared, the cause of more?

She rose out of the pool and heard the voice, Regina's, but could not be sure who else or how many of the other girls were with her.

"Don't drown, Hannah," Regina's voice carried from somewhere behind. "Would be such a shame if they found you face down in there!"

Hannah would not turn herself to face Regina.

"What would your Daddy do then, Hannah? Probably have them name the swimming complex after you, huh? Or maybe he'd shut down the whole school! You'd love that, wouldn't you?"

Hannah still would not turn, but raised herself out of the water to the side of the pool.

"Where you going Hannah, hanging out with all your friends today? Oh wait- you don't have any friends!"

Hannah went to the chair her towel rested on, grabbed it and head for the lockers, never turning.

"Little liars don't have friends, Hannah. If it wasn't for your daddy nobody would care at all if you lived or died- just like your mother."

Hannah was nearly in the lockers when Regina mentioned her mother. She stopped then, feeling as if she might breathe fire, and turned, but Regina had already gone. Looking

across the water at the nothing in the doorway Hannah
smoldered with darkest thoughts.

CHAPTER 1
PERSEPHONE

A chill seemed to crawl across the sprawl of Mount's Edge. Demeter looked towards Zeus for answer to their child, standing then toward the highest ridge of Olympus. Zeus' gaze held steadily there at the edge of Mount's Highest at his daughter Persephone.

"Persephone has a keen sense of these seasons," said Demeter. "They pass for her unlike they seem to for the rest of Olympus."

"You speak as if such sense were weak," said Zeus. "Persephone has strength."

Persephone could hear them both, listening past the wind sweeping the Mount's top.

"How many suns will pass that you watch our daughter suffer this way?"

Persephone wasn't listening to her mother and father anymore. Her senses remained in full depth on Sky and all that lay beneath. With her focus clear, Persephone, from that very edge of Mount's highest, held all Olympus in colorful, bright perfection- Sky and Sun she willed to embrace in an endless show of greens, blues and gold buried in rapturous Mid-light clouds streaming violet and rose.

At twelfth-year Persephone had first done this. Dreamlike streams filled the bounds of the land, fed from the Sky, and all Olympus, far and wide basked in abundance. In city, all bowed.

Now, at sixteenth-year, they still bowed at pass of the Goddess Persephone- Daughter of Great Zeus and Mother Demeter, but now many bowed from fear.

"Strength," Zeus shouted, smiling at the image of his Persephone, standing perfectly in sun's light. "Strength enough to sit throne of Nether," Zeus said low to Demeter. "My brother is wise to choose her."

His words burned inside Demeter, greater than all Nether. She believed Zeus' sacrifice of their daughter, at each Harvest's End, to sit throne, forced as Nether's queen, was too great a sacrifice- even if only until Bloom's Rising.

"Your brother chooses-," said Demeter, "but what does Great Zeus choose for Persephone?"

"She sits throne Nether," said Zeus, "so that all Olympus- from Mount to Valley's End may prosper- and Persephone is adored for it."

This Persephone heard.

They prosper 'til I take throne of Nether, she thought, looking out over Valley Olympus, dreamily watching the shadows of clouds swimming the land. But from Harvest's End on they were battered by Cold. All hurt, but none greater than Demeter for her child, Persephone- who hurt greatest of all to take throne of that vile realm.

As Persephone left each Harvest's End, Cold began from fury of Demeter, and would continue on, the Mother vowed, every sun's past for as long as Zeus allowed it- that their child be bound to her father's brother- Hades.

That first Nether-bound Harvest's End, Persephone cried, torrents of tears. The Valley flooded from them. One with child perished. Persephone begged. Only Zeus' hand could make her crying cease. It was the last Persephone wept.

Persephone grows cold herself, thought Demeter, with each sun's past. She begins to resemble Zeus this way. This thought shook Demeter.

Persephone's strength grows, thought Zeus. She will become the All Great of Olympus, Greater than Zeus himself. Persephone whips Olympus with a whiff of cold at mid-light, as if Sky All at her command.

"Much power sits throne of Nether," said Zeus to Demeter. "More than even Persephone knows."

Persephone strode nearer the edge of Mount Highest. She wanted no throne, and since her tears had drowned the one with child, Persephone wanted none of her power. Zeus said strength but to Persephone it was power- and each sun's past it grew.

She thought of each sun's past, of meadows on which she danced and from her feet flowers sprang, stepping with each memory toward the very edge of Highest Olympus.

"What does Great Zeus choose for me," Persephone asked, as if to the wind as she stood, toes at Mount's very end."

"Child," cried out Demeter to her, halting Persephone. Persephone let the wind pull back her tears and turned at edge to face her and father.

"Dear Mother," choked Persephone. "You and I both suffer so, for something I alone did. I am bound, by fruit of Hades to Nether- but to Nether, I vow now, I will not return."

"Persephone," called Zeus, "hold!"

"Forgive me, Mother," said Persephone, "but what choice have I?"

Zeus roared out, Great Thunder crackling loud over all of Olympus- so loud his words went unheard by her, but as she threw herself off Mount Highest, all Olympus- all Sky itself could hear Zeus cry out- "Persephone!"

CHAPTER 2
HANNAH

Hannah heard thunder in the distance.

She crouched on the tree limb. It was the oldest on the grounds. She'd climbed it as a child with her father watching on. Again it thundered and like a knife through the gray belly of clouds the sky opened up.

Rain, she thought. I'll feel rain one last time.

Then she thought of the note. It would be ruined in the rain. Still, they'd let him know when they found his daughter hanged that there was a note nearby that read: Daddy. She felt for it in the pocket of her jacket and began to cry once again. Hannah still reeled in her desperation to end it, but a numb came over her as it rained harder then.

She slung the rope around her neck, rising to her feet, bare, out on the limb, and without looking down to the ground where her father would always stand, Hannah sucked in a deep breath and leapt.

She barely had time to brace for the branch's pull- the jolt, when her ears filled fast, ferocious thunder-

She felt nothing, saw and heard nothing until...

... "Sweet, sweet Hannah," she heard her father's voice.

This is a dream, she thought.

A haze slowly lifted and Hannah was in her bedroom, still not sure if this was a dream. Her father laid his head against her hand then and she knew, and when he took Hannah's hand to his lips, she felt her father's tears and was sure it was real.

Her bedroom got bigger and that she was alive became settled. Then she saw the beautiful blue-eyed stranger standing solemn at the foot of her bed. For a moment, it was neither real or dream. Hannah thought it was the other side.

Laughing through tears, Hannah's father held her hand, joy racing through him and leaving him as laughter, so grateful to see his daughter's open eyes. He asked Hannah if she could speak.

"Yes," she said as a tear rolled softly to her pillow. "Who's that?" Her eyes hadn't left the stranger since they'd opened.

"Oh, honey," her father said. "This is the young lady that found you."

"Found me?"

"Do you even remember it, Hannah? That storm?"

"Thank you," Hannah said, still steady on the girl with the blue eyes. The girl, a soft, sun-kissed statue with eyes of pure ocean, held her attention on Hannah. She came close and told Hannah, "I am Persephone."

"Do you," asked Persephone. "Do you remember?"

Closer, Persephone's eyes took greater hold of Hannah. Had she ever seen eyes as brilliant?

"No," Hannah said softly.

"A tree limb struck you, honey. It broke off, from that old tree on the South wall, in the storm. Lightning brought it down. Persephone- she was passing through the edge of the property and found you."

"You're very fortunate," Persephone said, coming closer still to Hannah's side and then laying her hand on the side of

Hannah's face. Hannah felt a warmth that at last told her she was alive. Another tear slipped free, caught by Persephone's fingers.

"Persephone dragged the branch off of you," said Hannah's father, "carried you on her shoulders across the entire property, all the way to the house. Oh, sweet Hannah," he said, bowing his head to her hand again as the doorbell chimed.

Dr. Miraz was meeting them at the hospital. Hannah would be admitted and stay the night with a full battery of tests. Her father left the room to greet the EMTs.

"I have this," Persephone told Hannah, struggling for what to call the note she'd found. "I've told no one."

Hannah brought her hand to Persephone's where it still lay on her cheek. They both heard footsteps approaching.

"Forgive me, Hannah if it displeases you," Persephone said in near whisper, "but you'll not be dying anytime soon."

CHAPTER 3
DEMETER & APOLLO

She heard his footsteps far before she turned to face him. She felt him in the ground.

Demeter stood still in the vast meadows of the Valley, knowing not when or if she would see Persephone again, or where she had gone, but holding secret hope that her daughter would appear there, where so often as a child she played and danced. It was here- not throne of Nether, no- not even at Great Zeus' side on Mount Highest, that Persephone most found peace.

Demeter waited, her senses open to all- the wind, rays of sun, Sky herself, but nowhere was there sign of Persephone, only footsteps.

Demeter turned, already knowing from the sun's shine on the meadow that it was Apollo.

"Demeter," Apollo called to her and quickened his pace, reaching where the good Mother stood, and bowed.

"I come looking for Persephone," he said. "She is with you?"

"She is not," answered Demeter.

Apollo wondered then if Persephone were on her way, or perhaps with Father, but in searching Demeter's face he knew neither was true.

"Your head hangs, good Demeter. Tell me- where is Persephone?"

Demeter wanted to answer but could find no words and instead raised her eyes to Sky.

"Its many suns yet 'til Harvest's End," said Apollo, "many suns 'til she returns to that toil. Harvest only now stirs. Your head is heavy as if she has already resumed that wretched throne!"

"No, fair Apollo," said Demeter, "she has not. No, Persephone *would* not take Nether before Harvest's End."

"I beg you," said Apollo. "I beg you tell me."

"She is here Immortal," said Demeter, with eyes still to Sky, "here among all she holds dear, including you and I." Apollo bowed all the way to his knee and then spoke.

"Demeter, your words, true as they may be, fill me with sorrow, worse yet, with dread. I must ask more than this. I beg again- if you believe Persephone hold me dear, I must know where she be!"

"Fair Apollo," said Demeter, looking down at his troubled face, "stand before me."

As Apollo stood, his head remained heavy with worry. Demeter's soft hand lifted his chin. She looked at the fair-haired young God. His high-boned face, handsome, fought to shield his fear for what had become of Persephone.

"Apollo," she said, "I know that you love my daughter. I've known all along of these fields- your meeting place. It is where I once met with Great Zeus himself suns past."

Apollo took Demeter's hand in his.

"Is she Nether," asked Apollo. "She was stolen there once. Does Hades go back on his word to Zeus? I'll bring sun's light greatest on his Darkness..."

"No," answered Demeter. "Zeus may allow his brother Persephone's hand, as she is bound, but would not allow Hades take her longer."

"Taken by another then? On my word, Demeter- should harm have befallen her, I..."

Demeter's warm hand quieted Apollo.

"I cannot say where Persephone is, fair Apollo- nor can I say if harm has befallen her- but as you may ask yourself, could there be greater agony than that of the torture she's already known?"

"I will find her," flashed Apollo. "Good Mother Demeter, Persephone will be returned."

"Do as you will, dear Apollo," said Demeter. "Myself, I say no more, and for Persephone's sake, as these fields too have ears, you will say no more the same."

CHAPTER 4
PERSEPHONE &
HANNAH

She hated lying to her father but hated more the thought of disappointing him- a chance she could not face, and as Hannah told Persephone of her story, Persephone's eyes welled when Hannah's did, her throat became tight when Hannah's voice gave way to silent tears, and as Hannah shared with Persephone all that led her to the note and the tree and to feel so hopeless as to take her life, Persephone vowed to Hannah that her secret was safe.

"Thank you for not making me feel foolish. They say everyone thinks about it- about killing themselves. Even before this thing," Hannah said. "I'd thought about it once or twice. But after this- thing, this Spring Cotillion…" Hannah lowered her chin to her chest, shaking the memory away. "After that," she went on, "I felt suicidal just about every day. Have you?"

"Have I …," asked Persephone.

"Ever thought about it- about killing yourself?"

"Yes," answered Persephone, "but I'm not sure I could."

A friend, Hannah thought, a wonderful friend, and she smiled. Wishing the same, Persephone smiled too.

Mr. Molloy offered Persephone a ride home.

"Where do you live," he asked. She did not know how to answer. He saw this immediately and swept it away quickly. "You'll stay at the estate," Mr. Molloy said. "I absolutely insist." A runaway, he thought, but clearly this Persephone is special. It was settled that Persephone would stay the night, but it was at Persephone's insistence that she remain at the hospital with Hannah. Persephone suggested the empty bed beside Hannah as accommodation enough and Hannah quickly seconded the idea.

Mr. Molloy looked very tired. After Dr. Miraz got Hannah admitted, he examined Mr. Molloy and prescribed sleep and another exam the next afternoon. Both he and Miraz marveled at her feat, figuring Persephone's journey from the property's edge to doorstep to be nearly three miles, taking into consideration it was near night, in the rain, on uneven terrain, and with Hannah's full weight broad across her back.

"She's feather light, really," said Persephone.

They were alone in the hospital room. Persephone wore a hospital gown like Hannah's while her clothes dried on the tray table nearby. Her dress, so fine, soaked through in the storm—something it had never done in Olympus. She'd traded her soft cloak for Hannah's denim jacket, believing her cloak would keep Hannah driest, but her cloak too was soaked by rain. Persephone pulled Hannah's note out of the jacket's pocket and handed it to her.

"You read it," Hannah asked.

"There was no time, but – I didn't need to."

"Thank you," said Hannah, taking the note, "but enough about me and my problems. Tell me about you."

CHAPTER 5
HERMES

He sat not far from where the River met land, as deep in his thought as Styx itself.

With his palms down and toes up, he sat in the spot she always visited each Harvest's End, when time came for Persephone to resume her throne in Nether. She'd deemed it the edge of her soul- that last place of beauty on her path, where the rush of the river made enough noise to drown out that of the tortured beings ahead in Hades' grip. It was there, at the edge of Persephone's soul, where Hermes fell in love with her.

Her beauty was obvious, Hermes thought, but when she'd sit there with him and speak of the peace she found at that place along the river, Persephone became to him his heart's reason. Hermes fell wildly for Persephone, she being the bright-eyed daughter who, like he, could find beauty in such a place as Styx. Perhaps then, Hermes thought, she might find beauty in me the same.

He held these feelings, holding them as truly as he held his station there, but through suns past Hermes' affections continued to grow and his heart's reason at once became too it's damnation.

Madness, he thought. Is this my price, the torturing of *my* soul?

It became more than he could bear and he told her. Persephone, though kindly, told Hermes she did not share in his love and left.

That was Harvest's End three suns past.

Ah, it dawned on Hermes, *this* is my damnation! To guard his love's travels to Nether, to Hades- a cuckolding, Hermes thought, and yet he performed his duties and was her able guide through Styx to that grim labor.

Messenger, thought Hermes, why should fair Persephone- Daughter of Zeus, Queen of Nether, share in love with a messenger?

It was three suns past that, heartbroken, Hermes began to realize his own power. He ran Styx as if it's master. All that passed must first pass through him, and all that wanted safe passage would beg it of Hermes.

Hermes knew things before all others when it came to matters of worth- and no matter had greater worth along Styx than that concerning Zeus of Olympus and his brother, Hades of Nether- the two that ruled the realms on each side of the river. If words passed between Olympus and Nether, they were likely passed before Hermes, making the messenger powerful with secrets, but in three suns past, no power- no eminence achieved could rid him of the hurt in his heart over Persephone's love unreturned.

First, the ferry man brought news to Hermes of Apollo, his long rival, and of Apollo's journeys to meadows of the West.

Then came more, that Apollo goes to meet with Persephone, in the fields, just them two.

Hermes thought of crushing Apollo, with rage of Persephone and her consorting with another, and at his most hateful and heart torn Hermes imagined revenge on them both, but Hermes loved her still. She alone knew his soul innermost. She alone could ever be his River Queen. Persephone, he thought. My only joy save the river.

"Was Mother Demeter," said the ferry man, "that Apollo met in meadow last."

"Say when," Hermes demanded, or your voyage may become treacherous yet.

"You would threaten me," said the ferry man, "your friend Charon? Have I not been ever loyal to you swift Hermes? Was midlight, two moons past they met, sun after the Great Thunder afore. You heard the storm, of Zeus on Highest no doubt."

CHAPTER 6
MOLLOY

"Hannah's fine," said Dr. Miraz, and a relief swept under Molloy, taking him off his feet and into the seat of an armchair in the hospital lounge.

"Thank you, Tony. If something ever happened to her," said Molloy, "I- I just couldn't bear it, not after…"

Dr. Miraz knew what Molloy stopped himself from saying, not after Amy- the doctor knowing well the toll of his late wife's death on him.

"And I do," Molloy confessed to Miraz, "I do worry about Hannah."

"Hannah will never want for anything, Eric."

Eric Molloy had amassed significant wealth and had a vast hand in the quality of life for all in Stansfield. His family's contributions to the town, the Academy, to the general good of Stansfield gave the Molloy name great stature throughout. He had been Stansfield's Mayor as had his father before him, and having studied law had been its highest judge since. Hannah would want for nothing because she was a Molloy, heiress of Stansfield.

"It's time for you to rest," Dr. Miraz told Eric, "and next week I want to see you in my office for an official exam. It's been too long."

His honor changed the subject.

"Did they find anything out on Persephone?"

Hannah was not alone in her enchantment of Persephone, as Eric and Miraz too were taken by the brightness of her. Eric relished it at such a dark moment.

Dr. Miraz thought best to check and contacted Sheriff Cicero. The Sheriff ran just the name, Persephone, with a description and found nothing. Cicero offered to have one of his men sit at Hannah's door, he could do so himself, but Miraz decided it was not needed.

In the night, Cicero went to the hospital anyway, telling Miraz that he wanted a report taken of the incident.

"You can get your report in the morning," said Miraz, "when Judge Molloy returns."

Cicero was checking with nearby sheriffs in the three towns that border Stansfield. It looked like Eric was right- a runaway, but there seemed to be something mysterious about Persephone. There hadn't been much time for discussion of the girl though, or anything other than that of Hannah's care.

Miraz told Eric he had not heard anymore.

When he'd examined her that night Miraz thought her answer was strange. He asked the girl how old she was. Sixteen year- he was sure was her reply.

"Sixteen you say?"

"Yes," Persephone answered.

Miraz found her to be healthy and of superior body.

"She'll come home with Hannah and I," said Judge Molloy, "Right now, Persephone may be just what our house needs."

Miraz' mind raced for objection but could find none in time. Judge Molloy had decided.

Since his wife Amy had passed, Eric Molloy put very little thought into his own needs. He thought it would be impossible to ever marry again, but longed for his child to have a mother. At just sixteen Hannah had lost even more than he had, Eric believed, when Amy Molloy was taken from them. All Stansfield mourned with the Molloys but Judge Molloy mourned mostly for Hannah's loss of her mother.

Persephone was like a brilliant breath of fresh air. He felt that he owed his daughter's life to her.

CHAPTER 7
APOLLO

He was known throughout. His arrival in towns round Olympus brought bustle and to many delight. His feats passed in story and tale through, from old to young and on.

"Ho," said one. "Apollo comes and brings with him the Sun."

"Better said," added another, "that the Sun follows him."

"Maybe he'll play a song for us!"

"A song," someone chimed. "It's been Suns since he's carried his lyre."

Apollo had long given up the instrument, but that he once brought song remained in the memory of all Olympus, having heralded him once the God of Music.

He had not, for many Suns, drawn his silver arrows, yet his might remained fresh on the lips of all Olympus.

None could say they'd seen him pull the Sun itself, by horse-drawn chariot, east to west across the Sky, yet it's rising and falling came to be known as Apollo's doing.

"Like Sun," said one. "Like Sky itself, Apollo shows no age! Do you see his face, as a boy's still?

It was true and brought awe to see. Apollo- the mighty, the healer, the guide of Sun's light seemed not to grow old. The crowd that had come round took witness, praising his name.

"That's him," said one elder to a child, "Apollo, God of Light."

"Apollo same," asked the child, "That shot the Python Dragon from the Sky?"

"With a thousand arrows of silver," said the elder.

"Apollo the Mighty- Great Champion of the Sun," said another.

"What powers has he," said another. "Powers to heal as well. Remember the blind boy he once gave Sun's light to see? Truest of Zeus' blood he may be!"

"Mightier in ways," nodded the eldest. To this one, Apollo turned.

"Mightier than Zeus, do you think it so," Apollo asked.

"In ways, yes," came the answer, "In ways." Others agreed.

"If Zeus should ever falter," said one, "Olympus would do well to have Apollo in his stead."

"If Zeus should falter," said Apollo, "Olympus would need for very little- as Olympus would be no more."

"Apollo, Loyal Son," shouted one.

"You do the Great Father proud," rallied another, "and all Olympus the same. Thanks to you, for this Sun afore Harvest."

"The great son of Zeus can make a blind boy see," came a voice, "but what powers have he to heal a sickly tree?"

At this, Apollo's eyes darted through the crowd for the face from which such riddle came. Stepping through the rest came Hermes.

"Take leave," said Hermes, "all of you. I should have words with the Great Father's most beloved."

The group broke away, children being led by the hand from Apollo's side.

Apollo's dark eyes held Hermes tight until all had left. .

"You would do well to hold your tongue," said Apollo. "My arrows are sharper than your wit."

"Oh," said Hermes feigning surprise, "my talk of sickly trees- how cold of me? Apologies fair Apollo. I'd forgotten your Daphne, though see clear- you have not. I'll keep better hold of my tongue, and in turn advise you to do well in guarding your travels."

"What of my travels, Hermes?"

"Persephone," said Hermes, with a keen eye on those of Apollo. "You've been to see her, and most recent her Good Mother. News of it reaches me along the River."

"And what of it," challenged Apollo.

"To me, nothing," said Hermes, "but should such news reach past me to Nether- you'd find your arrows not as sharp as you believe."

CHAPTER 8

HANNAH'S ROOM

Hannah wept at the telling of it. With Persephone's hand in hers, Hannah recounted her heartache- over her mother's sudden passing, her father's depression, but had not yet spoken of the Spring Cotillion.

In the early morning hours though, as the new day dripped into Hannah's bedroom, where the girls had just begun drifting to sleep, the quiet of dawn was torn to shreds with a smash as shards of glass splintered away from the window frame.

A stone- tearing like paper through the window and into the room. Hannah shrieked. Persephone did not.

Her eyes lowered and she rose from the bed, stepping barefoot across the glass littered floor.

Hannah, sitting up in her bed, heard herself choke back another scream and listened- wide-eyed to the cracking of broken glass between the hardwood planks and Persephone's feet.

She bent down and grabbed up the stone in stride then reached the remains of the pane, fixing her eyes on what she found outside the window- a pair of girls, just at the mouth of the yard on the estate's east side, running headlong into the trees.

Persephone's eyes began to glow. Thunder coughed and charcoal clouds rolled fast in front of the sun, darkening the yard.

"Persephone," Hannah shouted.

White lighting flashed through the sky- finding Earth just past the tree line. At Hannah's holler, Persephone's eyes regained their true light, as if torches doused, and she turned toward Hannah.

Hannah's stare set low at Persephone's bare feet and their bloody path prints across the glass. Persephone followed Hannah's eyes and looked down. And now blood, she asked herself. First my gown is soaked by rain and now...?

"You're bleeding," let out Hannah, aghast at Persephone's ravaged feet. Hannah shot her look into Persephone's eyes.

"You didn't feel a thing, and that lighting- you did that," said Hannah.

Seconds passed silently then.

"I don't know what I'm saying," said Hannah, thinking back to the freak flash that filled the sky. "I just felt- like a tingle, like it came close or something. I had the same feeling when...the tree."

Ceaseless thanks, Great Father, Persephone thought relieved. A tingle- she's no notion!

"Are you alright," asked Hannah.

"I am," answered Persephone, feeling her own eyes strain.

"We need to go to the hospital. You need stitches. I'm getting my dad."

"I need nothing," Persephone said, "save for the pail I saw in the garden out front. I would myself, but..." she trailed off looking to her feet. "And in the pail, some water."

Bewildered, Hannah repeated the word- water, backing out of the room to fetch some.

CHAPTER 9
ZEUS & DEMETER

"Brother," she said with address to Zeus. "You and I will have words on this."

Demeter's tone was felt in the distance where wind rustled all in Olympus. Sky darkened gray.

Though not spoken oft, it was known that Zeus and Demeter were born of the same union -that of Cronus and Rhea, that Zeus sired the child Persephone with his kin-sister Demeter, and that while still child-Persephone was stolen to Nether by Hades- Demeter's kin-brother yet.

The Mother's rage had come to be known that first furious season of Cold- when Persephone was stolen to Nether and made Hades' queen, at just twelfth-year. That first, most angry Cold- through which the child was enslaved in that most wrenching of places, and through which all of Olympus and all North of Nether suffered in turn. Sky drew pale and Sun's light ceased to be. Cold dark fell over all for eighty and eight suns. Starved and brutalized by Cold, many perished.

Persephone was returned to Olympus but remained bound to Hades at each Harvest's End for another eighty and eight suns each, and Demeter's anger- the rage of the Mother North of Nether scolded her children all with Cold.

"She will be found before Harvest's End," said Zeus. "Land, air and sea will be scoured."

"And if not," asked Demeter.

"Persephone is born to this, Sister- of strength from you and I! Power enough to…"

"Power enough," scoffed Demeter as if to herself. "Zeus speaks of power but has none enough to free his daughter."

"Why free her from that which she is destined? Heir to all! Queen of Ever!"

"She wants only love," said Demeter.

"She has more," said Zeus. "She has adoration."

"If she returns, so be it, brother. But you will not send your hordes after," demanded Demeter.

"Hold your tongue to me!" Thunder roared as Zeus rose from his golden throne to his feet.

"I will once this is said," Demeter returned the force in kind. "In all of me I have always felt Persephone, but now I feel her no more. In her stead, I feel only- cold."

Zeus looked at Demeter's eyes, black as Styx's bottom. Before the Great Father, Demeter's fair skin went ashen.

"Go easy, Good Mother. She will be returned. The child only hides. Leave you now. Hera returns soon from the West."

Once Demeter was gone, Zeus summoned Hermes. The messenger quickly arrived and bowed humbly.

"Persephone's not been seen since the Great Thunder of last- frightened into hiding by me. You will keep listen- learn what you can of Persephone and her whereabouts."

"I will," said Hermes still lowered.

"You will do this with only word to me, and will give word on all you find."

"I will," said Hermes rising.

"You will tell none of our words," Zeus said drawing closer to Hermes. "You will tell none of this to Hades- or my lightning you will feel."

Hermes bowed again his allegiance.

"Great Father," he said. "Persephone is always at my watch and always of my highest affection. One did just speak of her to me! My head," Hermes said clapping it. "My head- oh yes! Apollo! He spoke of his meeting Persephone, and of Demeter the same. Be sure," he said head bowed, "I've told none."

"Apollo met with Persephone and Mother Demeter? Alone or both at once?"

"That I know not," said Hermes, "and with apologies I know not more. There is a tree though- along Styx, not far from the mouth of Nether. Persephone visits it. She's quite fond of the place. She's there now perhaps?"

"Perhaps," said Zeus.

"I can return with word next Mid-light."

"Do that," said Zeus, "and do tell Hades his brother rules well."

CHAPTER 10
JESSI & REGINA

Her scream was lost in the echo of the lighting, shrouded by the tearing of the tree limb from its body.

She screamed again as the limb tumbled toward her from above.

The branch- thick, thundered down through those below it, as if racing for Regina. A last limb in its path sent the falling one off course, sparing Regina harm but not horror from the bulky branch.

She stood there, at the foot of the tree, eyes wide on the branch that had landed just a few feet from her, its weight making the earth around her quake.

Just that one flash of lightning, from nowhere it seemed.

Stopping just before it, Jessi stood silent, watching- as if a movie, Regina's near battering.

Emotion coursing through her, Regina breathed heavy, fighting not to cry- her chest leaping. Jessi too labored for breath. Both ran track at Stansfield Prep. Neither should have been so winded, except this run had been off season.

Both girls stood waiting, each seven yards best from the fallen tree branch.

Jessi's eyes were to the sky, on watch for another flash, another branch or even a raindrop- but no sign of more storm arrived.

Slowly, the sun began to rise as Jessi looked back to Regina. Her hands on her hips, Regina's eyes had not left the massive carcass of broken tree, reimagining the horrid sound of its heavy thud in landing.

"That's it," Jessi said starting toward Regina. "That was the last time," she said reaching her, shaking her head. Her hand reached out, as if pleading at the branch between them. "That would have killed you."

Jessi searched Regina's eyes for some flicker, but in Regina, her hatred came back with her slowing breath. Regina began to laugh, finally taking her eyes from the ground.

"This whole damn town worships her."

"Just let it go," Jessi said.

"Let it go?" If the rock was in her hand again, Regina thought, she would throw it this time at Jessi. She twitched and asked again- "let it go?" Regina walked, stepping over the branch, toward Jessi.

Jessi knew already what Regina was about to start in with- the same as since the Spring Cotillion. Dejected, Jessi let go instead- of her hope that Regina might just forget about Hannah.

"All I've known for the last two years, all I've dreamt of," Regina said. "Evan and I are engaged," she said, holding forward her ring. "We are getting married. Stansfield will be *our* home!"

Regina swallowed back a cry.

"That bitch- ruined everything," said Regina, glaring wild up to the morning sky.

In her head, she imagined it all as she always did- her and Evan marrying, her becoming Regina Cicero then- wife of Evan Cicero, the Sheriff's son. Stansfield would celebrate such a union, carrying them well and for generations. Regina imagined their children and good life- the one she wanted.

"Nobody even believes her," said Jessi, "and I doubt anyone at school even knows!"

"It doesn't matter! You know what Hannah's little fairy tale could have cost me? Cost Evan, cost his dad?"

Regina turned, walking away from Jessi, stepping again over the heavy, dead limb.

"It'll be her under that branch before it's me."

CHAPTER 11
DAPHNE

Apollo received word that Zeus wished his presence on Mount Highest. He knew at once it was about Persephone. In this was his loyalty, and he began readying for conference with the Great Father, readying for whatever lay ahead.

If Hermes had news of those mid-light meets with Persephone, and news too of this last with the Good Mother, then by now Zeus too may know of them. If not from Hermes, Apollo thought, than perhaps from Demeter herself. At once, Apollo trusted none.

He went to his window, behind which his sickly tree stood.

It was simple then, Apollo thought, when all was music- before he'd ever taken up an arrow. Apollo kneeled at the sickly tree- a sorrow pulling him to her.

Daphne- turned to twisted thirsty root there by the Great Father himself. His sorrow turning to guilt, Apollo bowed- his large dark eyes damming shut the flood from guilt over his Daphne.

Zeus had, with his thunder and lightning powerful, turned Daphne into this tree for nothing the innocent had done, but as a strike against Apollo. To punish- yes, Apollo thought, but to save himself as well.

Apollo had become a champion in battle of Olympus, beloved by all for his valor. As his good favor grew, so did Zeus' watch on him- greatest when Apollo on chariot brought the Sun back to the Sky. Apollo was heralded by all.

Was then, Apollo believed, that Zeus made plans to crush him. Was then, Apollo believed, Zeus first feared Apollo his greater.

He struck Daphne, Apollo's truest of loves- leveling the warrior to humble knee at Great Father's side.

"I'd not strike my own kin-son," Zeus told Apollo, "and I'd not slay your Daphne- no matter my objections to her. You are a true warrior, champion of Sun and Sky! You'll not consort with River-folk. Apollo will have a true queen! It's your sun ahead- Age of Apollo! There is no time for your lyre and none for your grief. Daphne lives and is where she belongs, near her kin along River West.

Age of Apollo, Zeus called it all those suns ago, and Apollo had not aged since.

"I'll be taking leave of Mount Highest, Great Father."

"Leave, for how long?"

"Ever, Great Father," Apollo told him. "I am leaving Highest and all Olympus, for quiet solitude of River West."

Zeus knew Apollo was going to Daphne and knew from his kin-son's voice that he went to hide his heartache.

"Yes," agreed Zeus. "Go sit watch of the West where Sun settles, a wise post to keep watch from and close enough to Olympus."

Suns ago, battles many since, every wound Apollo suffered as warrior of Olympus cut not near as deep as Daphne's sad fate cut him.

And with hands his own Apollo built his place there, along River West, where just past his window sits a sickly tree that in sweet song to himself he still calls by name- Daphne.

"Striking me and not Daphne may have saved your good favors, Father," Apollo said as if to Zeus, still on knees at Daphne. "Olympus loved me. They'd have taken up against you Great Father. You denied me the love I cherished the most."

Apollo rose and shouldered his quiver, taking leave for his father's Golden throne.

Mightier than Zeus, he wondered. Could it be? And what had that village eldest said- In ways, yes- in ways.

CHAPTER 12
CICERO

Sheriff Cicero had gone to where Hannah had been reported found- by the tree on the South edge of the property belonging to Eric Molloy.

Cicero could find no evidence that pointed towards Hannah being struck by a fallen limb or for that matter of that tree being struck at all.

"Funny," said Miraz. "Hannah had no marks from it either. No breaks, bruises or even a scrape."

"The whole thing's funny," added Cicero, "like every other story that Molloy girl gives. And this other girl, the one you had me run- Persephone. What was she even doing there on the property? And just as this mystery branch fell? I think I'd like to ask her a few questions."

"I'm afraid that's not possible," said Miraz. "Not now anyway."

"And why's that?"

"She's gone home with Judge Molloy and Hannah."

Cicero shortened the distance between he and Miraz, lowering his large face into that of the doctor.

"I keep telling you, there's not an inch of Stansfield that's off limits to me. I ain't afraid of Molloy and I'm sure as shit not afraid of his little girl."

Cicero backed up, a finger to his badge.

"He may be judge," said Cicero, "but I'm still the law around here."

The law, Miraz nodded at Cicero and thought about that and all the law broken in Stansfield.

"It's been time enough," said Cicero. Cicero raised his chin and set his hat softly on his clean shaven skull. "I'm gonna pay the judge a visit."

Cicero drove, slowly and without hurry to the Molloy Estate, controlling his breath and listening to the radio- all he could think to do to relax. He'd been off meds all summer and hadn't had a drink for a year before that. The music helped, but still he was in Stansfield, where so much at once seemed to haunt and consume him.

Just relax yourself, he thought. Relax.

His cruiser curled along the curves of the winding road. He thought these weeks just before Fall were Stansfield's prettiest. Still, Cicero could not shake free from his mind's racings. Matters of late left him a wreck- and without his meds he thought of picking up the drink again. I'll have a drink, he thought, before I let Miraz medicate me again. Besides the antidepressants keeping his manhood limp, the doctor's sick intention, Cicero felt, he knew there was much worse Miraz was capable of with that prescription pad of his. He had the health and wellness of Stansfield in his hands and had the entire town seduced. Trust him about as far as I can throw him, Cicero thought to himself. Sometimes the Sheriff wished he had no ties with the doctor.

Cicero pulled to the front of the Molloy home and pulled from the visor an envelope. Grabbing his hat from the passenger seat, Cicero put it on and climbed the steps to the door.

CHAPTER 13
ZEUS &
APOLLO

Apollo bowed and before him stood Zeus- staring with his eyes icy at his son.

"Persephone," said Zeus. "You've seen her."

"Not in seven suns."

"You will find her," said Zeus. "Turn back the Sun's path if you must."

Apollo rose. "I will," he said.

"Your consort with her is of no use," said Zeus.

"I dare," said Apollo. "Persephone is of great use to me, Father."

"She is queen to him," said Zeus.

"And goddess to me," answered Apollo.

"Fool," snapped Zeus, turning his back on his son. "Return her by Harvest's End to me."

"You'll not send her back," said Apollo.

"You dare truly," said Zeus, turning slowly to face Apollo again. "To Nether she is wed- to Hades, and it will remain so."

"I will find her," said Apollo, to his knee again. "If I must retrieve her from Deepest Nether, Persephone will be…"

"You'll not set foot Nether," Apollo heard his Father say but did not turn back to contest.

Zeus fears Hades, Apollo thought. And Demeter, so strange in the field, as if wanting to say but still hiding something. His thoughts too great, Apollo uttered aloud- Hades! Who else could bring such dread? Hermes all but told the same. He knew in valley where Persephone was- Nether! My arrows not as sharp as I believe, Apollo told himself. The trickster will find deepest the mistake of his words.

Fear of all left Apollo as he began to head back to River West. I fear not Deepest Nether, nor Hades, thought Apollo. I fear not the Great Father himself.

At River West he sat solemn in Daphne's scarred shade, vowing before her to return Persephone from Nether, nay to Olympus.

"At any chance," he told Daphne and himself the same, "I will."

Many battles behind him, Apollo made vows to victory- against even the Sun, and praised his Great Father at each vow, but at this vow Apollo praised none and left, his quiver heavy, for the River Styx.

Along the River, Apollo recollected what he had nearly said to Zeus at Mount Highest, that he himself wished Persephone's hand, that as Hades stole her and made Persephone his bride, so would Apollo, the Champion, steal her back and make Persephone his. That union Demeter would bless. Cold would cease from her joy. Olympus over and Sky would delight. And of Hades- war! To free Persephone and free the army of souls from Nether! At any chance, Apollo thought, further along Styx by then. I will have Persephone- and then I will have my Daphne! Cruel, Apollo thought, that for all his power to heal he could do nothing for the sick laurel Daphne. But Persephone- Goddess of Harvest! Her touch alone will bring back my Daphne. For Daphne I will defy the Great Father. And again my heart will sing loudest.

CHAPTER 14
HANNAH &
PERSEPHONE

"There's no way we can be friends," said Hannah, "with you knowing so much about me and me knowing so little about you. Please," Hannah begged, "tell me about you."

Her feet soaking in the water Hannah had brought, Persephone started.

"I'm not sure where to begin," she said, swirling her feet in the calf-deep water, turning it pink. "I'm from a mountain top, Hannah- on the other side of the Sky."

Hannah sulked inside, trying to keep her eyes bright but suddenly Persephone's great brilliance had dimmed in that light of Hannah's reason.

"The other side of- the sky, you said?"

"My father rules there- like yours, he is strong, but of his love for his children, Eric Molloy likens most to my mother."

Hannah listened to the fantastic tale Persephone told and despite her greatest want for it, could not believe.

"All was perfection, Hannah- everything I touched bloomed, on breezes I could ride, free."

Hannah felt her heart break, feeling fooled in her fast attraction to her, and feeling differently now about Persephone. Still, this stranger, so beautiful and kind had an innocence- a shining star of a child's spirit that bound from her. Hannah thought the girl a bit crazy with it, her wild imagination, but found Persephone just as sweet despite it.

"I was very close to my mother," Persephone said, seizing Hannah's attention at once. "There was a time I never left her side."

She didn't say their names. They were brothers and sisters and friends, and Persephone went on with fantastic tales of them, in this otherworldly dreamlike place she said was on the other side of the sky, South of Nether.

"You're an incredible storyteller," Hannah told her. "You should write those stories down."

"Oh," said Persephone, "many are written, by the Scribes."

Hannah listened on, warming once again as first she had to the girl, thinking back to something her own mother once told her about being surprised sometimes at who you find a friend in.

Persephone told more of her mother, heralded by all, she sat one of the few thrones of gold.

"She's an adventurer, truest- free as all the wind and all are well in her harmony. A mother to all, really- but the same, is not to be crossed." Persephone went on of being forced upon, by her father's brother and of the rage at her mother's learning- rage coldest at that same season when the sun rose and fell fastest.

"I could bear it no more," said Persephone. "I believe you may know that feeling."

"Trapped," said Hannah, "that's how I felt- cornered. You?"

"Burned," said Persephone.

Of reaching Stansfield, from so far, Persephone told Hannah that she wasn't sure she would even make it there, but that she did not care.

At that, Hannah's chest had risen and held- her flashing back to her climb up that tree she meant to end her life from, and her own desperation from which those same words carried her, that of what happened she did not then care. Persephone had made it though, and somehow so had Hannah.

"It just sounds so crazy," Hannah said still looking into the bucket. "Are you crazy...like bat-shit crazy-crazy?"

"I don't know what you mean," laughed Persephone, "but I do enjoy how you say such things."

"What about this thunder and lightning stuff? You ride storms, is that what you're saying?"

"I can ride a great many things, if I think well enough about it."

"That tingle I had- did you make that lightning strike before? Or that bolt that hit that tree?"

Persephone thought hard about her answer, her eyes searching the dark water for her toes so as to avert them.

They both shook, Hannah stifling a scream when the doorbell chimed. Hannah hurried out of the room and down the hall, into her father's study for a look out the window. She could see the front drive from there. In it she saw his cruiser and sighed exhaustedly- Sheriff Cicero.

Back in Hannah's room, Persephone sat, starting to gently swirl and stretch her feet in the water. She must know, thought Persephone, but not now. She'd not bear to hear the story in full, least not her part.

Hannah felt a wave of cold roll through her as she listened at the top of the stairs to her father greeting Sheriff Cicero, straining to hear them. Sheriff Cicero made Hannah uneasy. She wasn't afraid of anyone as much as she was of Mr. Cicero- not even his son, Evan. It wrenched her stomach that he was in her home and trading good mornings with her dad.

Persephone heard Hannah's footsteps heading back to the bedroom.

"Who's here," asked Persephone.

Persephone's eyes searched for Hannah's but Hannah's head hung low, her hair covering her face.

In a voice as soft as a whisper Hannah answered, "Sheriff Cicero."

CHAPTER 15
DEMETER

The wind bent back the boughs of grain in the field as if bowing and receiving her- her path making great wave of the harvest.

In the distance, trees were full- their leaves beginning to turn and their fruit beginning to brown.

Demeter feared worst, true, but had strange sense too of yet another fate for Persephone.

Was surprise to her, Persephone's plunge- as was to Zeus, who at once filled the sky with lightning greatest, but was Demeter too who's shock rang out when her daughter leapt from Mount Highest. Again, Demeter feared worst, but decided the fates were now left to their way.

It could not be heard over Zeus' thunder, that at moment his bolts packed the sky white, Demeter- Mother of Harvest, brought crippling wind, swift as Zeus struck, swift as the child leapt…

Was a time, many suns past, that Demeter too, like her daughter, was taken by storm- into thunder, Sky a wall of white- and at once came great horror. But what horror, wondered Demeter, has Persephone not as yet seen?

Harvest was fast upon Olympus and the valleys, from stretches wide cross Sky busied in wait, stopping to bow to the ground though, as Demeter passed.

"A plentiful Harvest on us," said a gatherer "would be praised to you, Good Mother."

"Praises too," said another, "to the merciful moon. If night must rule at Harvest's End, let it rule and again be gone. Brave it we will- Olympus!"

"Olympus," they rallied back around her as Demeter continued on through the valley, as if none had fussed about her. Still another fawned further on, falling to knees before Demeter.

"Greatest of Mothers, we cry- on each star in Sky we cry for Persephone. Praises to her, Demeter- and praises to you!"

Demeter had been struck, though none is written of it, by thunderbolt of Zeus. Scribes knew none of it- Demeter running and off Mount Highest and at once afire, with nothing beneath her feet, nothing within reach, and a burning so great her screams could not drown out the thunderous clap of lashing flames.

Lashing Demeter's thoughts then was Zeus. If by wind at my command I ushered my child to such wrath as Zeus' lightning, perhaps it best if Persephone resigned to that place rather than be torn so savagely between these two. Demeter wished for none of it to be true, for Apollo to somehow reach Persephone, steal her away, live well at River West and lament no more those things taken away. Apollo the Strong, thought Demeter, Mover of Sun, take her and defend her as you would Olympus. That would be best, Demeter herself resigned, but still the Mother of Harvest could not be settled with her daughter not in sight.

Demeter reached the valley's edge and brought down on it light rain. Demeter closed her eyes and the rain began falling heavier. Steal myself away- with no word, she thought, even to Zeus. Let him feel me, for all suns forward- Ever Cold. It would be, perhaps, the end of all.

CHAPTER 16
CICERO & MOLLOY

The Molloy Estate had ample room for live-in help but none had been employed there since Amy joined the house. When Eric and Amy took residence of the Estate, Amy insisted they have no domestic help. They had cleaners and grounds men, but none with quarters.

Hannah could clean her own room, do her own laundry and help prepare meals. Amy believed one should answer their own door for it to be their home. Eric gave Amy every allowance on such matters of the family.

In community, Amy took charge as well. The Molloys had always given greatly to Stansfield, but it was Amy who became most charitable, and perhaps most beloved of all Stansfield's women. There were those who contributed much of the Judge's good favors to his wife's good favors, content in thinking a vote for Molloy was a vote for both Eric and Amy.

In her memory, each year since her passing, Judge Molloy offered to an outstanding Stanfield Preparatory student the Amy Molloy Grant- a full tuition gift to Academy.

Cicero smiled, sliding the envelope from his shirt.

"Evan's application," Cicero said, "the Amy Grant. You said to bring it by."

"I did," said Molloy, taking it and smiling apologetic.

"The kid's really working hard, Eric. He's pulled those grades way up. I leaned on him good. He's not only gonna captain swim, he's doing a triathlon in December."

"That's fantastic," said Molloy. "He's really come into his own."

"Well, thanks," said Cicero, "and thanks for that," he said pointing to the grant application.

"I'll get it to the board," said Molloy.

Cicero pulled off his sunglasses and stepped into the doorway closer.

"Eric, I heard from Miraz. He says Hannah's fine but I felt I should check in on you guys."

"She is fine," said Molloy, "just needs some rest now. I should be doing the same."

Cicero's foot and shoulder nearly inside. "The other girl," he said. "She's here?"

"Yes," said Molloy, "also resting."

Cicero leaned closer to Molloy so that his voice would not travel. "You sure it's a good idea- her being here? What do you even know about her?"

"I know she saved my daughter," said Molloy, "and right now it's all I need to know."

"I've been to the edge of your property, Eric- that's what's on my report, the tree on the South wall was struck by lightning and a limb fell. But there was no limb, Eric. I didn't find anything that jives with a falling branch story."

"What are you trying to say, Sheriff?"

"These are kids, Eric. What were these girls even doing out there?"

Molloy tightened his robe and reached for the door.

"Sheriff, these are all very good questions, but as I said, we're all resting this morning."

"Eric," said Cicero. "I just thought you should know. I know your daughter's had a rough time of things- better than anyone around here, I know. Kids can go down the wrong road. You gotta stay on top of 'em- get tough sometimes. Evan don't dare tell a lie to me- not me or any of his elders."

"There's no need for me to doubt what Hannah tells me Sheriff, but thanks for your concern."

"Well," said Cicero. "I'd still like to speak to this Persephone, Eric."

"In time," said Eric starting again to close the door when Persephone appeared just behind it.

"I'm not here to cause trouble," she said. "My name is Persephone. Ask anything you like, Sheriff. I will answer."

CHAPTER 17
DARK TREE

Hermes journeyed back, twisting along with the River, following with keen eyes Persephone's path to Nether.

He'd done this before- imagining her steps, light on the ground and imagining each spot or object that might draw her look, but this time Hermes retraced Persephone's trek with even greater attention.

It was perhaps Hades greatest power that Nether could be reached by very few without forfeiture of their freedom to leave. But even of those very few, there were those who Hades did trick into turning over their souls to Nether- Persephone counting as one.

Most reaching Nether were soulless, punished into madness and enslaved to Hades' Dead Horde.

Hermes stopped at a marshland field, sad and dressed in brown yellow of Harvest's End. He spied Persephone once bathe her feet at a pond there.

Hermes had swift passage, by way of Styx, to Nether and was rare to have passage all number of places. It was said by some that Hermes the Trickster had passage to secret places- this, true or tale, became perhaps Hermes greatest power.

It was said too, behind the hands of some, that Hermes far reaches and swiftness held strong his post between Hades and Zeus. None challenged Hermes to take his post as Messenger for fear wrath of both Hades and Zeus at once. It was Hermes, they agreed, that would be messenger. None dared challenge it.

Further down River- Hermes sat in shade from the oak of a muddy wood- resting easy in the folded roots where Persephone sometimes nestled.

From there, Persephone once painted the most wonderful picture in the Sky, reaching far from Styx over Olympus- making miracle clouds roll slow across great fields of gold and blue, Sun settling in beds of violet- tolling to all Harvest's End. Some wept at sight of it and at the sacrifice of Persephone's voyage Nether, Hermes counting as one suns past.

Hermes rose and hastened, further down River, to another stop of Persephone's- the Dark Tree of North Nether. Sharper air there tightened cold his flesh to him.

He stopped then, less forty paces from it, eyes at once on the mass of black at the Dark Tree's feet- laying there as if a dead mare fallen from Sky.

He hastened to the mass, slowing and circling around it to see it in full. A tree limb- large, long and around, lay heavy on the ground- it's weight having torn into the dirt beneath it.

It lay my size times five, Hermes thought, his eyes moving the limb's length. At its center, he noticed something tied round it. Hermes looked up into the tree then, looking to see from where and what height the branch had fallen from when from behind him he heard a voice call out- Ho!

With slight jump Hermes turned- Apollo!

Regaining, Hermes watched Apollo walk toward him, he smiled and sat perfectly where the Dark Tree's limb had been tied.

"You won't sit long," said Apollo advancing.

Hermes pushed his heels beneath him and his hands into the branch, but did not rise from it. Paces more, Apollo drew his bow, from back to at aim, and sent arrow fast Hermes' way. Hermes sprang but the arrow found its mark- through Hermes' pouch, carrying and lodging it in the ground past the branch.

Apollo turned his shoulder, Hermes already behind him.

"Apologies," said Hermes stepping back. "Allow me space to greet fairest son of Zeus. Allow me to bow."

Hermes bowed, pulling from his ankle his dagger. Apollo set, a second arrow trained at Hermes' heart.

"Words," said Apollo. "I've message for Hades."

Hermes looked Apollo in the eyes then darted them fast past him to the fallen branch at Apollo's back.

"Words," said Hermes, bowing slow to sheath his dagger.

CHAPTER 18
REGINA'S ROOM

Regina and Jess had showered. Both girls felt better then, there on the cool of the balcony off Regina's bedroom.

Jess wondered still about the freak surprise of lightning just an hour before. Regina was drying her hair when Evan texted that he was there. Balcony, she texted him back and soon he was inside the home and coming through her room. With Evan was Cam. Evan turned Regina to him, kissing her deeply.

"Where you been," Evan asked.

"For a run," Regina answered

Cam sat beside Jess. They traded nods hello.

"I'm gonna go," said Jess.

"Why," asked Regina. "Hang out."

"Yeah, hang out," said Cam.

"I'm just real beat," said Jess shaking her head. "Got some stuff to do later."

"Call me," said Regina before Jess told them goodbye and left.

"What's her problem," asked Evan

"She's just stressing," said Regina. "She applied for the grant."

"My dad's hand-delivering mine today."

"I told her you were getting it, Evan. I don't know why she even bothered."

"Hannah's dad's taking care of it for me," said Evan. "My dad's sure it's mine."

Regina's face got hard. Folding her arms she swung her back to Evan.

"What" asked Evan, "-what'd I say?"

"You could have just said Judge Molloy was taking care of it, but you said Hannah's dad." Regina resisted the urge to go on, snapping a fast glance Cam's way.

"Cam," said Evan. "Go. Be back in an hour. We'll gym it up," and with that Cam left.

"You do that on purpose," Regina went on. "You know I don't want to hear her name, least of all from my fiancé's mouth!"

Evan moved close to Regina again, taking her by the waist from behind.

"I'm sorry," Evan said with a soft squeeze and breathing in the scent of her thick waves of brown hair. Regina's hands went to Evan's, holding them there on her hips. "I won't say her name again," Evan whispered.

"Yes, you will," Regina decided and broke his hands off of her.

"School's about to start, Evan," she turned to say to him. "Everyone's gonna be looking at me- looking at us! Just looking like- is it true? Evan- the whole class thinks you and Hannah…"

"They do not," Evan shot. "They think she's a fucking freak- and a liar!"

"Not all of them," argued Regina and then lowered her head as if to hide tears.

"The girl's a head case," Evan said, softer now. "Little Miss Depressed playing her sad little flute, dressed all in her gloom and doom black on black- crying on the school shrink's couch." Evan lifted Regina's head, offering his best sincerity. "She's a head case," he said. "No one believes her." Evan kissed her then- soft and gradually deep. Regina let herself be held by him, softening her lips to his.

They moved with the breeze from the balcony to Regina's bed and the cool coming into the room made light and easy those next moments between them. Regina forgave him.

CHAPTER 19
APOLLO &
HERMES

Apollo handed a silver arrow to Hermes.

"Take to Hades this arrow, a message that Apollo is on the look for Persephone. If he stands in way of it, that arrow you hold may find its way to him. If he has hold of her, tell Hades this arrow he will feel surest." Apollo set the arrow across Hermes open palms.

"Persephone," Hermes asked. "What's this you say of her, held Nether?"

"Don't fool with me Messenger," said Apollo. "I know your tricks."

"Apollo you will listen. Forget all of you and I before. If Persephone is threatened you will have full allegiance of this messenger! If Hades holds her, true he will feel this arrow- by Hermes' hand! It was her true that I saw. I thought my eyes deceived!"

Hermes turned, holding the arrow in his fist, and went fast for his path.

"Hermes," called Apollo, halting him by hand. "She is there then? You've seen her Nether."

"I thought so," said Hermes, "from the cracking wind that came of a screaming soul past me. At once the soul radiated to me, as if the wind itself carried her along- at once I thought of...No! Great Father, no! Could it be, hidden past me, that soul was our Persephone? Great Zeus, I must..." Hermes turned, fleet-footed for his path. Again, Apollo stopped him.

"Hermes," Apollo said, "passion plagues you! What blow could you deal Hades? He'd crush you to ash and punish Persephone the greater."

"True," said Hermes, hiding his eyes to Apollo's chest, "but the Great Father himself Hades could not crush! I'll get word to Zeus at once. Nether will shake from his lightning. Zeus will champion Persephone back and crush Hades!"

"Will he," asked Apollo.

"What say you, Apollo?"

"You know as I, Hermes, how all suffer at Harvest's End, Persephone's exile Nether- and Zeus allows this! Command it he might as well!"

"True," said Hermes, "true."

"Zeus' lightning may shake Nether," said Apollo, "but I'd crush the wicked whole of it with the Sun."

"But Zeus," said Hermes. "I'm to Mount Highest, to see him by end of next light. Dare I say none of mistaking Goddess Persephone for a soul off to Hades' torment?"

"I ask you do this then," said Apollo, "Take this message to Hades first, before you're off to Zeus- this silver arrow to Hades from me- and have look yourself for that screaming soul."

Hermes bowed slightly. "I will, Apollo," he said. "And to where do you go?"

"Further downriver," said Apollo, "maybe trace still of Persephone can be found."

"There's a troubled spring she visits," said Hermes. "It cries out in endless agony but if its wail can be withstood it tells of all it sees. It's told me before of seeing Persephone."

"I'll demand it say fast if it's seen her, or soul alike pass."

"It's this way," said Hermes, his arm out and away from the Dark Oak, and with haste Apollo was led to a path Hermes assured was fastest.

As they walked, Apollo kept hand ready for his bow behind Hermes.

"This is as far as I go," Hermes finally said. "I'm off to deliver your arrow. Have you words for Hades with it?"

"No words from me to Hades," said Apollo, "only my Silver."

CHAPTER 20
THE STONE

She charmed him, as she had all of those whose glance became look became dreamy gaze into her eyes, and Cicero fell to catch every word she spoke. Eric Molloy stood in like hold of her, listening without doubt of sincerity to Persephone, standing so sweet before them in a short robe of Hannah's. And by then, upstairs, in wonder still in her room, Hannah too was charmed. In Persephone, Hannah at once felt something magical and strange to her, and something at once kindred.

Hannah felt this take hold just moments before, with Persephone still in the room with her, toweling dry her feet, the rosy gray of the water- and there being not a mark left of broken flesh. Silently, Hannah stared at Persephone's feet while she dried them, and the room stayed silent until Persephone broke Hannah's trance and spoke.

"You're not bat-shit crazy," she told her, sweeping to knees beside her and taking Hannah's hand.

Sun broke through the room and with it a gust of cool morning. The stone that crashed through the window hummed giving light vibration to the floor. Hands held, they said nothing in that moment as Persephone's shimmering eyes slowly turned from their sky blue to a dark violet hue of pure night.

Still entranced Hannah heard birds then and the sun had drawn back and Persephone's robed back was at the door and then gone. Hannah was high from it. Behind Hannah's closed eyes Persephone remained, begging gently of Hannah to help her.

"My name is Persephone. I'm sixteen. I had documents but I lost them in my travels. I've come a long way to study at Stansfield."

In her room, with the stone still humming and softly glowing on the floor, Hannah's thoughts and Persephone's became as entwined as their hands had been. As clear as Persephone could hear it, Cicero's voice resonated in Hannah as if she were downstairs with them.

"And where are you from, Persephone?"

In Hannah's head her mother's face flashed. Hannah smiled and thought of the place.

"Norway," Persephone told Cicero.

"Norway," repeated Molloy. "My wife was from Norway."

"You have family here, Persephone? Where are your mother and father?"

"I have no family here," said Persephone. "My father is home. He would accompany me but has much responsibility- in Norway."

"And your mother," asked Cicero.

Hannah's eyes, still closed, fell heavy.

"Dead," said Persephone.

"I'm sorry," said Molloy, reaching her shoulder with his hand.

The grant, thought Hannah.

"The grant," said Persephone. "I would like to apply for it- the Molloy grant, and study at Stansfield Prep. I had an application- for the grant and the semester, but I lost those too. I lost everything. Do you think there is a way I can still apply in time for Fall?"

"Of course," said Molloy. "We'll get you new applications, of course!"

Cicero's attention snapped back and his eyes followed fast to Molloy and then back to Persephone.

"The Molloy Grant," Cicero said. "My son's applied for it too. That's a tough one."

"Is it?", said Persephone.

"It is," answered Molloy. "It awards students of great well-roundedness- in athletics, the arts, in academics..."

"Also in the community," added Cicero. "My son, Evan- he's raising money for the Athletic Department, doing the Charity Dash. We're always doing all we can for Stanfield."

"Yes," agreed Molloy. "Well, home is where the heart is, am I right? Are you an athlete, Persephone, any sports for you?"

"Sports- oh yes," said Persephone. "I run. I swim."

"And where you gonna be staying, Persephone," asked the Sheriff.

"She's staying here," said Molloy, "and right now I'd like to get off my feet, if you'll excuse us, Sheriff."

Cicero started to leave but stopped at the door asking one last question.

"What's your full name, honey- Persephone...?"

Hannah searched in her mind while Cicero waited for an answer. Persephone too thought through names- flicking at them in the ticks of those seconds before she answered. The sky darkened quickly and a growling thunder sounded. Softly, Persephone said- Hades.

"What was that," asked Cicero. "Hayes?"

Yes, thought Hannah fast, Persephone Hayes.

Cicero seemed to take note of it with a nod and was then leaving. Setting his hat on his head he looked out over the front lawn to the sky.

"Was that thunder I heard? Heard some just before I got here too, and now- blue skies and sunshine. If we aren't having the craziest weather lately," said Cicero.

Upstairs, Hannah's eyes opened and from her window, the stone in her hand, she watched Cicero drive off and with the sun stretching again into her room, Hannah's head cleared hazy into the summer day.

CHAPTER 21
THE ARROW

Hermes moved swift, so as not to be seen, downriver past the marsh's atrocities and trappings, unharmed on the treacherous terrain along Styx.

Tales were told of Hermes by some, as tales led to such in late drunken moon, oft in places on ridge of the Valley, of the Great Messenger's skill with hand and dagger and other means of battle. That he'd slain in his travels, of loyalty to Zeus, was well known, but that the Messenger had slain when not in service was spread thin- and without favor.

Hermes' paths allowed travel so fast was said of his ease from Nether and back that he could run faster than fire. He ran, jumping over jutting ground, springing cross cool stream and lower ground where none could be seen- dodging traps and haunted trees, fighting free of beast and lost soul alike. In his pouch, between obstacles he'd make sure he'd not lost the arrow- Silver of Apollo.

At once, a wild goat beast surprised Hermes- lost from its hill and mad with hunger. The goat beast charged closer than Hermes would allow before he snatched at its horn and curled it to the ground.

Hermes held the goat beast grounded, his knee falling heavy on the wild thing's side and its jagged right horn held with force to the stone of a swamp's bed.

The thing spat and snarled with hate and Hermes yanked at the beast's horn, twisting its neck until the creature went silent.

Hermes, his knee on the neck of the beast, reached his dagger and breathed- seeing then his breath begin to show from cold. He breathed easy- steady in keep with the goat beast's own. Steady were the thing's eyes up at it, and steady it was- the dagger in the hand of Hermes.

A cough came from the beast as Hermes' hand came down, plunging his dagger into the side of its skull. Hermes rose, standing over the slain thing, watching better his breath like smoke in the dim. Hermes wiped clean his dagger with the hood of his cloak, but held it to his eyes before sheathing it. What final tale of Hermes it would be, Hermes thought, if ended by beast with Apollo's Silver in his pouch, lost to all but those who are lost themselves in this place between places and times.

Greater cold came slow upon Hermes, like the fog crawling over the swamp, to his face and hands first. The Last Tale of Hermes, he thought, likely only a line in this Tale of Apollo's Silver.

On Hermes went, with little more delaying him, to Deepest Nether, where at once demons hissed to greet him, fire leapt from broken ground as if to seduce him with its hot light, and to Hades throne the Messenger was led.

Hades sat, head low, lit by fire from the crown of his throne, and the shadow of him cast down his risen rock like giant black spider.

Through smoke, Hades lifted his eyes just enough to see the Messenger's and said his name as if in answer- Hermes!

The Messenger rushed to bow and presented from his pouch the arrow.

"Silver," asked Hades.

"Of Apollo," answered Hermes. "He makes this arrow his message to you, Your Darkness."

"Then come," said Hades, fire rising and clapping between them. "Deliver your message."

CHAPTER 22
MIRAZ & MOLLOY

Molloy relayed the rest of the story to Miraz in the doctor's office- the conditions by which Persephone said she'd arrived, alone and penniless but determined.

"And I'm determined to help her," said Molloy, "determined to see her succeed here."

Miraz saw clear that in the short time she'd been staying with the Molloys, Persephone had breathed fresh and welcome life into the house.

"Deep breaths," said Miraz, pressing his stethoscope to Eric's back.

"Hannah's taken to her too," said Molloy, "like a sister. She helped Persephone fill out her applications and register. I know you've had concerns about Hannah," he said to the doctor. "I thought you'd like to know how well she's doing since the accident."

"And again," said Miraz and pressed his scope over Molloy's heart. Molloy breathed fully, expanding his broad chest.

"Eric, I'm still concerned about Hannah," said Miraz, slipping his scope around his neck and taking Molloy's wrist for pulse. "And I'm concerned about you, too, my friend. I'll be frank, Hannah's accident concerns me. Forgetting Persephone was there- she's a separate concern, what was Hannah even doing out there the other night?"

"She was playing, I assume, her flute. She doesn't like to play indoors."

"There was no flute," said Miraz. "Cicero had a look at the scene- no flute, and no broken tree branches."

"What are you saying, Tony?"

Miraz took his hand from Molloy's wrist. "I'm saying you're heart is racing. You're in otherwise excellent shape for your age, Eric, so I'm not gravely worried, but it's your blood pressure as well- and the excitement of all this. I'd really like to see you on a very small dose of something."

Molloy leaned back as if to rest on the examination chair in Miraz's office. "Hannah's got another appointment with that psychologist at the school."

"How many times has she gone?"

"Just twice."

"I know Miss Helling, she's wonderful, but Hannah may need more attention than that."

Molloy thought. "Well," he said. "I think Hannah knows best what she needs. Still, since that last bit of trouble, I worry it's the same. That she doesn't ask for help because she's the judge's daughter, Eric Molloy's kid! I worry she sees an expectation that maybe she doesn't think she can meet. There's a pressure in being a Molloy in Stansfield- a pressure to being in Prep, with her flute, and swim and her studies."

Molloy stopped, took a breath and nodded. "Alright, Tony," he gave in, "I'll take that prescription."

"As I said, a small dose, and in your health, likely temporary." The doctor snatched his pen and pressed it to his pad. "Sixty days, your Honor," Miraz said, writing it as if handing down a sentence. On the corner of the prescription Miraz scribbled a star and wrote the word "hold" beside it, then stuffed it into his shirt pocket.

"I'm on my way to the Chemist's," said Miraz. "I'll drop it off. Start it a-sap."

"I will, thank you Tony. That's a help. I've got to get back to the house to meet Ted Becker for an estimate. Hannah's bedroom window- the wind slammed it shut and smashed the pane."

"Wind sent my trash cans down the street the other morning too," said Miraz, "weather's been so odd."

"Something to do with the atmosphere, says Persephone- bright girl."

"So she'll be staying? And attending Academy?"

"Yes," said Molloy. "Well, officially she's awaiting acceptance, but I've written her a letter." Molloy stood, sliding his arms into his shirt.

"How will she afford Academy? You said she arrived with nothing."

"Well," said Molloy, "she's applied for Amy's grant."

"And you're awarding it to her?"

"Well, mine is only one vote. The Grant has a committee, after all- it's a year's school and board."

"It's only that the Grant has such prestige, so fast. I know it's become competitive."

"Well," said Molloy, "these things have ways of working out."

"Still," said Miraz, "I'm concerned about Persephone- and her staying with you. You are the judge, His Honor Eric Molloy- and you know very little about her. I just don't want to see you be taken advantage of, Eric- you or Hannah."

"I know."

"That being said, if either of those girls experiences headaches, trouble sleeping, nausea or change in appetite..."

"Okay," said Molloy, "We'll call."

Tony Miraz had practice at dealing tough matters to Judge Molloy. He'd given Eric the news of his wife's passing and was as sensitive in telling him just months before that his daughter, despite her word, had not been assaulted by Evan Cicero. Tony Miraz knew well what Eric meant of there being a pressure to being a Molloy in Stansfield. It was the same pressure he used to render Hannah silent on the matter as after thorough exam Miraz determined there had been no assault, that she was only embarrassed, made uncomfortable by the Cicero boy, but had not been physically harmed- and could spare her father, the Ciceros, the town whole the ugliness of a scandal such as this in Stansfield.

"I'll talk to your father," he told Hannah after that exam. "Maybe that's easier."

She sat silent there, in her gown, on the examination table.

"You'll see," said Miraz. "This will all go away. We were all kids once. We all told stories."

CHAPTER 23
DREAM OF DEMETER

Breeze eased soft over the golden brown meadow-Demeter's work at bending nature to her will. She stood there, feeling inside herself for something, in the field's abundance, even if only a fragrance on a breeze, of Persephone. Instead, inside her, Demeter found something else for comfort. As close as the Great Mother had been to her daughter, it was there, in her desperate want for word from her, that she fell at once closest to Persephone. Over the field, endless cloud-splashed blue washed over Demeter's grim recollection of her dream. In this meadow of gold, where Persephone felt so herself and at peace, Demeter considered her vision.

Moon before Persephone's departure, Demeter had dreamt so bizarrely of her. It woke her with a tremble, seeming so true, that in this dream Persephone told her mother farewell and stepped into pure white.

At this dream of Persephone, Demeter throttled awake, the white of it still clouding her eyes then awake, seeing last her daughter glow amidst truest light. Demeter held back a scream in waking, and now, thinking of it there in the field, Demeter wept-heavy that her dream foretold and heaviest that Persephone be fated as such.

A gust of wind whipped through the field wild, blowing back Demeter's fair hair and gown with sharp chill. Her tears dried to her as all bristled and blew, bent from the wind. Cold, thought Demeter, and the ground dried and began to tighten.

"Ho," she heard. "Good Mother Demeter!"

"Apollo," Demeter turned surprised.

"Words on Persephone," he said bowing. "She may be Nether, stolen once more by Hades. Hermes told of a soul he thought the Goddess in disguise."

Demeter's eyes seemed to retreat from it. "Is there more?" Apollo stepped through the field closer.

"I will return her, but ask one reward of you."

"Reward?"

"I will retrieve Persephone, true," Apollo said, hand to heart, "but ask favor in return the same."

"Ask," said Demeter.

"Persephone's hand," said Apollo, "to share with mine as Sun King and Queen."

"And what of Hades?"

"Hades be dealt with," said Apollo.

Demeter stepped closer and took Apollo's palm in hers. "I allow you her hand."

Apollo smiled, with a love new for the Good Mother, and without her saying, Apollo believed her aware as he of the depth of such vow to return Persephone and from Hades take her hand- depths as deep as darkest Nether and as gaping as all of Olympus.

Apollo embraced Demeter and Demeter allowed him, holding in thought her dream once more, and holding in too what she thought true- that Persephone was not stolen Nether, but rode lightning to its end- North of there.

CHAPTER 24
SPRING COTILLION

Hannah recounted to Miss Helling everything that had occurred of late, with much devoted to the arrival of Persephone Hayes, but of the truth, Hannah said only what had already been said, that a tree branch had fallen on her in the storm and that she was found by Persephone. They'd reached the end of their session.

"This is quite a change since the last time I saw you," said Miss Helling. "It sounds like you've really responded positively to this young lady being in your home, and I think it's great- but, we've not touched on any of the things we had started on last session. I'd like to schedule again with you- for next week."

Hannah adored Miss Helling, finding in her a genuine care that was mother like, and because of this she struggled to speak to her- and struggled to tell Miss Helling she did not wish to attend another session.

"I just have a thousand things to do before school starts," she said. "I'm motivated though. I'm even helping my dad arrange Persephone's documents. I'm thinking about law."

"Hannah, that's really wonderful."

"Summer's almost over. Last time we met, I – I didn't want it to end, but now? I don't know- I feel like- like I'm ready for Fall, like anything could happen and I'm ready."

As Hannah said it she reflected fast on all that truly had happened, and withheld that which most wanted to be spoken- that she'd set out, that Persephone's first night, to end her life.

Across, Miss Helling smiled, sorrow eyed and softened Hannah.

"Maybe that Tuesday after Labor Day, Miss H," Hannah said.

"I'd like that, Hannah- same time?"

In Hannah came an urge to put her arms around Miss Helling and she did, arms to her in a way that left Miss Helling feeling as if parted with and worried.

There had been excitement in Hannah as she'd not seen before though- a hope she'd not seen since she'd known the girl. Still, she worried that while Persephone may have helped Hannah turn a corner, she may not yet be out of the woods of her grief and depression. They'd spoken last session about medication, but like her father, Hannah preferred not to take pills. They'd spoken too last session of meeting with more frequency, after Hannah first spoke about the bullying. Hannah never called it that, and never referred to them as bullies or mentioned them by names at all- just as classmates, and through her telling, Miss Helling recalled, she did not cry. Nor had she cried in that first session, nor mentioned by name "this boy".

This boy, Hannah said, taking great pause before going on about the night of the Spring Cotillion. She never said his name, and in that delicate desperate hour that evening, told Miss Helling only that he touched her.

"This boy, at the Cotillion," Hannah said. "We danced, and then later we were alone. He touched me," she said. "I told him to stop."

On this alone, Miss Helling told Hannah's father that a medical doctor should be seen- at once.

Hannah resisted therapy. Her grades had only slightly faltered since her mother's passing, but she brought them back up. She trained hard in the pool, but all summer had considered quitting the team, if only to escape the cruelty of Regina, since Cotillion.

Regina had bad-mouthed Hannah to all in the Stansfield class she saw through break, and had many of the girls believing Hannah a liar and a whore, who tried to steal away her boyfriend and then made vicious accusations of him when he rebuked her. Many still from school, believed it could be true- that Evan Cicero assaulted Hannah Molloy the night of Spring Cotillion. This though, to Hannah, was no consolation. All this Hannah told Miss Helling, with no mention of names, but when the girl came back, having seen the doctor, deciding to forget that she'd been molested, and at once Miss Helling guessed the boy might be the Sheriff's son.

"I just decided to forget it," Hannah told Miss H. "The doctor said I was alright. I just want to put it behind me now. I don't need a big mess for me and my dad. I don't want any trouble. Really," she said, "I'm alright."

Hannah left and thought of going right back inside, begging Miss Helling's kind help. Alone, Hannah cried as if a storm inside her was being emptied, and a wind passed with force enough to make leaves shake and flowers lean. Wiping away tears, Hannah looked up and down the wind's path and wondered, with all that suddenly seemed so unreal, if she would ever be alright.

CHAPTER 25
HERMES IN DEEPEST

Dark furies sprang from walls, each screaming with eyes of fire and hate.

Silver of Apollo- Hermes swung with the arrow, still in his hands, batting back each wailing soul suddenly upon him.

Hermes ran, with arrow cutting his way, fast from Hades' rage- the tortured cries of his army, taking form as if from Hermes' feet, and the hideous scream of Hades himself- his battle cry curdling loud.

But Hermes ran fast and fought off the horde, with his Darkness conjuring endless ambush, past all to a passage Hades himself did not know- away from Deepest Nether. Hermes kept at speed, by ways none knew or would ever imagine, but in no direction- only away from there.

Furies of fire, with whips for me- but why, Hermes wondered. He looked close at the arrow, still in his hand. Apollo's Silver- Hades saw its shine and commanded at once his hate at me!

Hermes was gone from Nether, his feet swift from the three-headed dog at guard its Gate, but not yet sure if he'd return to Styx. At a shady space between rot-wounded trees, Hermes stopped and pulled from his pouch the rope.

None knew of these trees but he and Persephone, and now, feeling safe enough to slow there, Hermes held the knotted rope he'd taken from the fallen Oak branch.

Others knew of the Dark Tree, but only Persephone had ever climbed it or ever touched its limbs. It was her, Hermes thought of first, when he saw the rope wrapped round the branch. The rope was heavy and browned from age but felt in Hermes' hands strong still to bear weight.

"I know a passage you do not."

Hermes remembered then Persephone saying so, while stopped on way Nether, and now had notion of which passage Persephone meant. She'd been asking the Messenger of his journeys North of Nether. Was then, Hermes remembered, she'd spoken of a passage he did not know. But the rope, he wondered. What of that? His heart rose with it though- that no matter the rope's meaning, Persephone's knot could only be for Hermes to find. And if she'd sent the rope true, then she was somewhere within reach.

But first, Hermes thought, to Zeus. He tucked away the rope and held to his back, by his Messenger's pouch, he carried Apollo's arrow. Apollo, Hermes wondered- had he fooled the Sun King again or had the warrior deceived him, and wondered on about who's mistrust might be greatest, his or that of the mighty Son.

Upon Hermes at once was a winged dog, frothing and starved to near bone. It lunged and sent Hermes sideways, off his feet. The mongrel latched its jaws on Hermes' arm, near his shoulder, but Hermes, still falling, flung himself free with a shove of his feet, sending the dog sprawl past him. Wild, it whirled back, but not before Hermes dagger was drawn. He slit the beast full under as it flew at him.

To Zeus at once, Hermes thought, to Mount Highest-ahead of Apollo.

CHAPTER 26
JESSICA JORDAN

Miss Helling had just one other appointment that day, her third that summer with the girl- Jessica Jordan.

The girl came without her family knowing, had called herself to make that first appointment. When Miss Helling asked, Jessica Jordan couldn't say why she wanted to talk to someone.

"I don't know, Miss Helling. I have lot of friends. I just…"

"It's ok," Miss Helling said, seeing the girl shy away. "We can talk about all of that."

"Thanks, Miss Helling."

"Call me Miss H."

"I'm Jessi."

Jessi told Miss H plainly how she hated her best friend, hated all of her friends. Snobs, and from them Jessi had to work hard at hiding the hardship that had torn apart her home.

She spoke plainly about the burden she felt she'd been on her parents and that they struggled to keep the family in Stansfield- and Jessi at Prep.

She spoke plainly about her best friend's boyfriend making advances toward her, what an asshole he was, and how he cheated on her friend all the time. Jessi let him kiss her once, but he tried very fast to take things further. She shoved him off.

"I'll tell your girlfriend," Jessi told him.

"You would," he answered laughing, haughty to himself before leaving.

"It was a lie though," Jessi told Miss H. "I'd never tell Regina."

"Do you like this boy?"

"No! He's a fucking pig."

At this Miss H laughed. "I'm not sure I like boys at all," Jessi confessed the last time they met.

"Why wouldn't you tell your friend that her boyfriend was unfaithful?"

"She'd deny it," said Jessi, "and make my life even more miserable. It's like, I can't even stop hanging out with her. If I ever told her I was hanging out with someone else, she'd freak."

"So," Miss Helling said, "she'd freak, then what?"

"Then, she'd make sure I didn't have another friend in this town."

"How is this girl so dominant over things?"

"I don't know," said Jessi. "She just has this way, and a wicked temper. Everyone's like- afraid of her, but they act like, I don't know- like phonies or followers or something, like- like me."

Jessi spoke plainly, telling Miss Helling that she hated herself. Eyes soft with great sorrow, Jessi blamed herself for her parents' divorce.

"I applied for the Molloy Grant this year, but I have no chance. Even if I had the grades and activities, the daughter hates me."

At this Miss H laughed too. "I can't see how anyone could hate you, Jess. You're a bright, bright young woman."

"Well," Jess said, "I can be pretty shitty sometimes."

Her phone buzzed and lit beside her. Jessi grabbed and read to herself the text- From: Regina CALL ME.

"Speaking of shitty," Jessi said, "my best friend." Jessica's thumbs worked fast to reply- 15 min. "There's no escaping it, and she doesn't give a goddamn about anyone but herself."

"What about finding new friends?"

"Where, in Stansfield? Town's mostly assholes."

"That's not true," said Miss Helling.

Jessi had no response and sat quiet a moment before her phone buzzed again. From: Regina 10!

It buzzed again. From: Regina ☺

"I wouldn't care if I didn't find new friends, really. I wouldn't mind being alone. I hate being popular. I think I'd live with my dad. I think he'd like to leave Stansfield, start over too. Maybe we could if it wasn't for my mom. It'd kill her if I lived with my dad. I don't know," said Jessi exhausted, "maybe I'll just run away."

CHAPTER 27
MOUNT HIGHEST

Apollo never went to the screaming springs. Once he was sure that Hermes had left for Hades, the Sun King made straight for Mount Highest.

"Father," he told Zeus, "I ask your full forces."

"You've found Persephone?"

"Known she is," said Apollo, "to be held by Hades Nether."

"Known by whom?"

"By me, from the Messenger" said Apollo, "and now by you from me."

"Hermes? He is due here," said Zeus. "I'll hear it from him true."

"You will not!"

Zeus stood from his throne and straightened his beard and then his gaze at his warrior son. "Speak more, Apollo. Tell all."

"You'll not have words from Hermes, Father. The Messenger betrays you. He plots with Hades- to keep Persephone bound and keep Olympus Ever Cold. I ask once more," said Apollo, "your forces full behind me- to win our Persephone back and end Hades' reign once and all!"

"Slow, Apollo," said Zeus. "We will not hasten to upheaval…"

"Hasten we must," Apollo challenged. "if not with your forces, Father, then of my own- and Demeter's."

"Not without say of me!"

"With or without, Father," said Apollo. "I steal Persephone back, and with vow of Demeter- I keep her."

Zeus stepped nearer to Apollo then, his teeth fighting to unclench as he spoke.

"You think you've might enough to challenge my brother? Champion of the Sun you may be- but of Nether and all of Darkness, Hades prevails- ever."

"And you'd give Persephone over to him," she said from their side, and both Zeus and Apollo turned fast their attention to see her- Mother Demeter. "Apollo offers to lead forces against the whole of Nether."

"And fail at it, he would," said Zeus. Apollo, eyes icy at his Father, said nothing- only glared cold.

"I give him my full forces," said Demeter. "Wind and more, all at Apollo's ask."

It was the Great Father saying nothing then, replying only with his look- eyes ice white and relentless under bent brow at Demeter. For all Zeus could do to push the historians ink his way, the Great Father could not dodge that the title itself- Great Father, was oft said with other meaning.

It was impossible for Zeus to hide from his scribes, or any in Olympus, that he'd sired so many daughters and sons with so many a consort. To Zeus, such was his duty to Olympus and All that his children should rule ever. Each would have power their own, and of child with Demeter, Zeus had greatest hope for an heir truest- and was born Persephone.

Zeus, thoughtful, returned to his throne.

"If Hades must be removed from his seat, then removed by me it will be."

From throne, Zeus looked at both Apollo and Demeter, standing cross the other, his beard high as if with suspicion. That moment went on, frozen by the Great Father's words and curious look at them, Apollo and Demeter, eyes up to his Golden Throne- silent, until yet another voice startled all three.

"Know this first, Great Father," said Hermes, "and you, Good Mother," then bowing. All turned, surprised to see the Messenger, and in his hand- Silver of Apollo. "This arrow's been in deal Nether," said Hermes, tossing it to the floor between them, "as sure as Apollo's been in ear of Mother Demeter."

CHAPTER 28
DISCOVERY

She'd seen for herself the girl's mysterious powers- to heal, to meld her thoughts through the air to her, her close kinship with nature, and in nature they stayed on the spread of the property where Hannah demonstrated to her new friend her own abilities with her flute, playing piece after piece in the cool shade of the poplars for Persephone. Persephone clapped lightly, smiling wide.

"I adore your playing," Persephone said. "I had a friend who was quite musical. He'd have such eyes for you."

"All this crazy weather lately," Hannah said, laying in the grass and looking up at the slow-rolling puffs of cloud across the light blue sky, "it's something to do with you, isn't it?"

Persephone, on her back as well, answered with pause. "Well…"

"Tell me about it," Hannah said, "the other side of the sky."

"Well," Persephone said, "it's much to do with the strangeness of nature, that's true. If you look close, when Sky is clear enough, there's a great many things you'll see, and much of it begins on the other side- on Olympus."

"Olympus?"

"Yes," said Persephone, "the mountain I come from."

"Mount Olympus," said Hannah, "from Greek Mythology?"

"Mythology," said Persephone, "I don't understand."

At once Hannah was up and standing over Persephone, holding her hands out to her.

"C'mon," said Hannah, "we're going inside."

"Why?"

"I've got to show you something."

They ran in the house and up to Hannah's room.

"Look," said Hannah, clicking her mouse to the website. On the screen before her, Persephone saw images unbelievable- where scribes all these suns ahead still told the tales of Olympus, and still clicking on word after word, Hannah raised to their view tale after tale, told and retold, some she knew as but rumors and secrets yet page after page of them turned before her- in all of places, Persephone thought, the Writings of Mount Highest, there left to this Earth?

"Hold," said Persephone, herself reaching for Hannah's mouse hand. "There."

A drawing of the Olympians, like fruit from a great tree, with branches drawing them to their places, and Persephone's attention went fast to that fruit at the tree's top.

"Father!"

Hannah looked, reading the name, and then looked away from it to Persephone to ask.

"Zeus?"

At Persephone's urging, Hannah continued through page after page, with stunning illustrations of them- the Gods and Goddesses of this place, Ancient Greece.

"But so much is untrue," said Persephone, "I think I've heard of this other place- Greece, but Olympus has no place by such name, and the telling..."

Hannah could see the pain on Persephone's face as she read, at times with such hurt her breath shortened- at times with such contempt she turned her whole body away from it.

"What is it, Persephone?"

"It's the lies- the twisting of truth. Hannah, this mythology is from the other side, but it's not at all..."

Persephone's thought vanished as her eyes then found, bold blue letters, the link- reading Demeter and Persephone.

"That's you, isn't it?"

"Yes," said Persephone, "and my mother."

All color seemed to leave Persephone's face, then white as the screen in front of them.

"You don't have to read it."

"I do," said Persephone, and took Hannah's chair closest to the screen. Hannah left her, sitting instead on her bed while Persephone read what the writing left of her story. After some time, Persephone rose.

"I've read enough," Persephone said. "I'd really like to go back outside now if we could."

Hannah rose from her bed and at once embraced Persephone. Hannah held her.

"And please," said Persephone, "do bring your flute. I'd enjoy a song now."

CHAPTER 29
MOUNT
HIGHEST II

"Apollo," said Zeus, "why does Hermes hold your Silver?"

"He sent it as message," said Hermes, "to Hades. Its true meaning he would not tell."

"Who then, Apollo, has betrayed Olympus?"

"Was warning, Father," said Apollo. "I'd already learned Hades hid Persephone! Hermes told tale of seeing her, disguised as a lost soul!"

Zeus turned to Hermes. Demeter walked to the Messenger's side. Apollo stood, his chin bent with disbelief at seeing Hermes there.

'Words, Hermes," said Zeus. "Speak them true."

"I did see her," he said, "or a soul I believed Persephone. It moved past me so fast I could not collect any toll, on a wind so strong, so cold. The soul's hair was dark, as raven's wings, nothing like Persephone's, but on a storm of wind…" He looked Demeter squarely before saying to her, "If it were her true, I know where she's gone."

"Lies," said Apollo. "The Messenger sides with Hades!"

"Lies of Apollo," said Hermes. "Hades tried to trap me there. Your Silver, Apollo- was at sight of that his Darkness turned his scorn on me."

At this, Apollo stood silent, his eyes reaching like hands to cover the mouth of Hermes.

"No more words," shouted Demeter, "unless they are of my child!"

There was silence then, with all being spoken to and by all four in only looks and stances, hardest being Demeter's deep eyes on Zeus.

"Apollo- if Persephone be stolen Nether, return her."

"On Olympus," said Apollo, "I vow it."

Apollo stepped strong, off at once, but was stopped by Hermes. "Passion plagues you, Apollo! I wonder what it is that enthralls you to war with Hades."

"It is by Persephone that I am enthralled, Hermes- the one who will be my queen," said Apollo, looking to Demeter on saying so.

Hermes paused, thinking of letting the warrior go off to battle, wanting him to be crushed and end all in doing, but after pause could not. Again, to Demeter, Hermes faced.

"She is not Nether," Hermes told her. "Fooled I may be in that flash of soul swept across Styx, but I believe Persephone is elsewhere. I believe she be- North of there."

Demeter turned, as if away from the notion, her eyes down, shadowy with dread.

Of all that was possible of Zeus and his kin, it was Hermes with power greater than all in way. Passage of time, and the lapses in existences, left these realms- of Olympus, of Nether and of North of it most distant. The distance though seemed of no matter to Hermes in his travels, giving him power like no other to traverse these times, with precise mark, and transcend time itself- be both past and future at once.

"Say where, Messenger," spoke Apollo. "Father, I will ride steeds through Sky wide to reach her, with the Sun itself my chariot"

"Your Sun won't get you there. Where she is, none of Olympus has been, not as I have. Great Father," said Hermes, bowing, "I am with honor, Persephone's champion." Hermes turned and bowed to Demeter. "With honor, I will retrieve her, Good Mother. Lightning may get you North of Nether, Apollo- but only I can get to Persephone."

"Go you both," said Zeus, "to North of Nether!"

Sky darkened deepest gray, lit only with streams of faint violet, and a low thunder growled in the wind off Mount Highest.

"No more words," Zeus rang and thunder ripped through the clouds. It crackled still as a wicked white flash pierced the gray.

From the floor, Apollo lifted his arrow.

From his pouch, Hermes took the noose. He held his hand out to Apollo, reaching for Apollo to take it. Apollo shouldered his Silver and reached at once for Hermes' hand. In those steps, each looked the other close, never leaving the other's eyes. The steps were few and Apollo had Hermes' hand- or he believed! Hermes gripped the noose tight- and fast was gone.

"And now," asked Apollo- arms out to Zeus, "and now do you see how Hermes betrays?"

Zeus lowered his beard to his chest. "He will return, with word- or more, Persephone herself. You will stay here at my side- to ready us both for Hades."

"No," said Demeter. "With Hades you will contend."

Demeter turned from both and strode to the very edge of Mount Highest, to where she'd watched her daughter throw herself. Looking skyward, Demeter said, "Apollo- stand here as I do," and the Sun King traded places with her.

"Zeus," Demeter said, "Great Lightning- as that when Persephone leapt."

Thunder hummed first, and then grew to a steady rattle.

"Return Persephone," Demeter yelled over it, to the edge and Apollo. Behind her, Zeus stood with his arms slowly rising. Demeter steadied her eyes at Apollo's back, and a slow, full wind blew strong at it.

Apollo fought it and braced- not letting Demeter's gust send him off.

"Stand free," yelled Demeter. "This is all chance we have."

The rattle became quake in its wait with Zeus' arms outstretched to sky- and then Demeter commanded it, shouting, "Now," and Zeus brought firm his arms down. A great white flash filled the gray fast and allowing it, a fierce wind carried Apollo to it.

Thunder sounded like Sky had been torn from it and at once Apollo was gone.

CHAPTER 30
ASSEMBLY

The tree on the edge of Molloy's estate stood full, looming like a shadow over her in the rain. It poured over Persephone as she panted, cooling her shoulders and back. The mud and grass beneath her hands and knees felt relief to her too, but still she heaved fast for breath. Lightning's End, Persephone thought, turning her head slow to her surroundings. I am there.

And still looking, from tree to falling rain, to ground again, Persephone then saw the fallen limb- arm's reach from her, and looking closer, Persephone saw the girl pinned beneath it.

It was the rain falling then that for the first time brought Persephone back to that moment when she'd reached North of Nether- finding Hannah.

With Hannah beside her in the backseat of Eric's car, Persephone felt a chill from the memory brought back by the rain on the road before them.

"This will be your first real look at the Academy, won't it Persephone?" She nodded and said yes. "You both look just beautiful," Eric said, stealing another look in the mirror as he drove.

There was all that, in rain just like this, of the rope, and the note, and the girl's very end. Persephone paused only to consider sending message back to Olympus, took the rope from the girl's neck and with hands placed firm on the branch, Persephone closed her eyes, bent and lifted. Strength of my blood, she thought, willing the wind within her for might. The branch held high over her head, Persephone held all her force back inside her and willed again, the Sky this time. Like her journey there, Persephone did not know what waited, but with blood of Zeus hot inside her, she brought down from the clouds lightning her own. Thunder sounded in three short pops before the bolt found its mark- the branch in Persephone's grip, and on being struck the limb was gone.

Eric drove slow, the rain showering lighter then over all the beauty between the estate and campus where they head. Music came easy through the speakers as Eric rolled on through the morning. Persephone sensed something uneasy in Hannah as they got closer to Stansfield Academy and considered all the girl had been through, both since and before her arrival.

The rain began to wither and Persephone's mind went again to the tree, where with power withering too, Persephone knelt, placing her lips to Hannah's and breathed what she could inside her, with only hope for certain. Persephone removed the girl's jacket, removed her own robe and wrapped Hannah in it, carrying her off- hope again her only guide.

A sign read: Stansfield Preparatory Academy next right. The sun broke and bounced off the wet road and suddenly all was bright. All would be at Assembly, like the morning- bright and showered with full colors vivid everywhere the eye fell. As it seemed always to the Molloys, another perfect Stansfield day would mark the end of summer.

They stepped out of the car and into the sunlit crowd, all headed to the Assembly, beautifully garbed and in good spirit, making lines to Academy Hall.

All eyes seemed on them and for certain on the new girl. Hannah was most aware of it all and thought, from somewhere in the parade of people, she heard whispered- Persephone.

"You alright, honey," asked Molloy.

"Yeah," Hannah said, "you know I don't like these things."

Eric put one arm around his daughter, smiling, and offered Persephone his other.

Many smiled and greeted the Molloys as they neared the Hall, smiling too at this new girl. Persephone at once felt welcome, but at the Hall steps she felt peculiar, sure at once that Hannah was suddenly suffering.

"Judge Molloy," said Cicero. "Hannah, I think you both know Evan."

Hannah's eyes went to her father's feet, as if prodding them to keep moving, without even a glance up at the Sheriff and his son.

"Yes," said Molloy, "good morning, boys," as they continued to the steps.

As they reached the top step all felt warm again as good mornings and hands were shared by all in front of the wide Hall doors.

"Oh, a rainbow," said a young lady near them, "over there, past the stables." Heads here and there turned that way.

"Look," Hannah said to her father, "it looks like it's right over the house."

A rainbow, Persephone thought and turned fast her eyes that way, her head gently falling to her shoulder, arching as the rainbow was from the Sky to the ground. Smiling, Persephone took Hannah's hand as they sat inside, the rainbow in great view through the Hall's windows.

CHAPTER 31
RAINBOW'S END

At Rainbow's End, Hermes set foot, having ridden the sky-washed trail to this place, the knotted rope leading him, as if by hand.

He sensed at once that she'd been there and thrilled, his eyes wide across the lay of this beautiful new land, that Persephone was near.

Few in Olympus knew of rainbows and in dank of Nether none were ever seen. Hermes knew all of rainbows and much else of things North of Nether.

He could reach here with ease, by way of bends and branching tunnels beneath the river- but to find Persephone, Hermes needed the noose- his conduit to her, and this place- Stansfield. Still in his grip, the noose led him again then, away from the tree through lush green, tree-flanked fields and grassy hills. Then, with hardly a cloud or a sound to forewarn came a fast flash of white hot light, somewhere behind the dwelling ahead of him. Hermes stopped, with urgent listen, and eyes scanning the land wide for sight of lightning. With the sky indifferent, Hermes went on. At the dwelling, he stopped behind thickets and watched the two.

In Olympus they were called mortals- souls yet taken from their flesh, said the scribes of Mount Highest, but Hermes knew there was more to be said of them. Hermes had been round them to know much of them and this realm they claim. Hermes knew them as they were called here- as men.

The noose suddenly pulled and it whizzed fast past his face- an arrow!

Hermes rolled down to the ground and came up with dagger drawn.

"Ease, Messenger- I'd not have struck you." Apollo came, heavy-footed across the lawn toward Hermes, reaching round to his quiver.

"That arrow," said Apollo "was a message." Apollo quickly set and drew another.

"Hold," he told Hermes.

With just steps between them, a bell sounded deep from somewhere beyond. Hermes looked fast that way, realizing the rope was drawing him toward the heavy clang.

"Hold even your eyes, Hermes," Apollo said, his eyes piercing as if arrows aimed too. "My armor withstood much of the agony, but still, I'll not take such scalding to follow you, only for you to…"

"That's class assembly," one of the men- the older, said to the younger, and only then did Apollo take notice- mortals beside them, taking his eyes that moment from Hermes.

Hermes held, Apollo's Silver still trained.

"Knees," ordered Apollo, bringing his arrow's tip to the steely eyes of Hermes. Hermes knelt.

"You'll not win Persephone," Hermes said.

"They're ringing the big bell," said the man. "They must be starting things." The two pulled and set a ladder at the side of the house.

"Not you alone," Hermes went on. "Not without guide."

Apollo breathed heavy and held, his arrow at Hermes, thinking uneasy that Hermes spoke the truth.

The younger man climbed the ladder and started up toward a window and the other rounded the home, as Hermes and Apollo held both out of sight.

"I'm chance only," said Hermes. "I'll hold, but I won't kneel," and he rose to crouching feet.

CHAPTER 32
TOLLING

"There's more to this place then known, Apollo. At once you'll see advances these mortals have made. Dull as the Scribes have written them, they are brilliant- and I am familiar most with their ways," said Hermes. "They call this Earth, and these mortals are called men. We are North of Nether, yes Apollo- but also many suns from ours."

Thickets shrouded Hermes and Apollo from the men, who cleared glass from the frame of Hannah's bedroom window.

"There's more, said Hermes, but not now. Now, you have to do as I say. We need those two men."

They watched close, creeping toward the house with the two distracted by their work, and soon Hermes and Apollo were nearly upon them.

"You'll seize this one closest," said Hermes, "with force-but without a sound." Apollo drew and targeted his bow.

"Once he's downed, take his garb. Hide yours with your armor, in the brush."

"What of the elder?"

"I'll see to him," said Hermes.

Hermes head out of sight, gone from Apollo, round the house the way the older man had gone, and drew up the hood of his cloak.

The one closest to Apollo climbed up the ladder, toward the other, talking of the rain having passed.

"Glad the sun's out," he said climbing. "Like to get a last tan before summer's over."

From the older man inside the house, working at the frame, there was no reply and when the younger man looked up, no sight of him. The one climbing reached the top and yelled out- Dad!

Apollo let loose his arrow which found fast its mark, splintering to tinder the foot of the ladder, sending the young man falling hard, air leaving his lungs in a grunt as he reached ground.

Hermes, hood pulled back, peered out from the window. The young man did not move below as he lay on the lawn beside the ladder.

"Without a sound," said Hermes, "did I not say?" Not waiting for Apollo's reply, Hermes nodded to the young man on the ground. "His clothing- wear it."

Inside, the old man lay, his face painted red and his mouth pulled open with terror, sprawled cross Hannah's bedroom floor and Hermes standing over him, hood over his lowered head, having frenzied with fear the mortal's heart-arresting it.

Hermes knew much of this world, and in turn this world knew much of Hermes- not only as his Olympian name was written, but by another name with legend its own. In this place, he was known to man as the one who came to rid the dead of their flesh. In this place called Earth he was known most not by the name Hermes but as- the Reaper.

Apollo wrestled free the young man's garb, leaving him bare-chested and with one less pair of shorts. Apollo then removed his own attire and dressed.

"In there," said Hermes, back outside and unhooded, pointing to the open rear doors of the work van. "Set that young man."

"Hermes! You- you look-," startled by him, Apollo could not find the words.

"Yes," said Hermes, "I have paled. You'll find your own, Apollo- this Earth is not as we know it. Now fast, conceal the man where I say."

"Where you say," snapped Apollo. "Say this- or conceal him yourself! Where is Persephone?"

"West of us," said Hermes, "where the bell tolled. There's not time for more, Apollo! The ladder too, it must be set right," Hermes said, dragging the young man himself to the van.

Laying him inside, Hermes back out of the van, but before his head fully rose out he was struck!

Over Hermes then stood Apollo, still holding the ladder he'd bludgeoned the Messenger with. Apollo stepped over Hermes, sliding the ladder into the van, then lowered and lifted Hermes up- laying him inside beside it.

CHAPTER 33

AWARD

"Welcome, everyone, to Class Assembly."

All in the Hall applauded Miss Helling, who stood at the podium onstage, applauding as well the tremendous spirit of Stansfield and the Academy's turnout.

"There's so much to get to, so let's get to it," Miss Helling said. "Presenting this year's recipient with the Amy Molloy Memorial Grant is our former Mayor, his Honor- Judge Eric Molloy."

Again the Hall thundered with cheer as Judge Molloy moved to the podium. Many rose from their seats. Cicero, standing, whistled and clapped. Molloy, smiling, waved them all back down to their seats, tall at center stage over all.

"The Amy Molloy Memorial Grant is awarded on the very ideals my wife wanted upheld for the Academy and for all of Stansfield. This year's recipient represents all Amy's ideals of a well-rounded and benevolent citizen- a standout on campus and in community. This year, on behalf of the Amy Molloy Foundation and its board, I am proud to award Stansfield's Evan Cicero."

The note in Hannah's denim jacket had only begun to get wet when Persephone found it, placing it in her cloak,

wrapped round Hannah, keeping it dry. Now she'd seen the boy-
Evan Cicero, whose act led Hannah to write it. Persephone
sensed huge weight on Hannah's heart at even Evan's name
being spoken. Hannah, her eyes aimed at the air above the stage,
clapped with the rest for him. Persephone reached for Hannah's
hand as the boy accepted his award. Hannah looked first to their
hands, then to Persephone, and smiled- smiling wider as the
applause again rose and with Persephone then smiling back.
Hannah, finding strength suddenly from Persephone, decided
then, to herself, that she would be alright after all.

"Congratulations to you, Evan," Judge Molloy told the
boy before then addressing the Hall. "We're gonna see Evan
again later on in today's Charity Dash. We will also be welcoming
a new addition to our campus with a tree planting- a gift from
Stansfield's newest addition! It gives me great pleasure to make
the gift of a special award to this very special new student. This
year marks the very first Young Ambassadors Award and its
recipient comes to us from Norway and will be joining our
Greenhouse team this Fall. Please, everyone welcome- Miss
Persephone Hayes. Go on, stand up Persephone!"

The crowd burst into applause, this time at the
announcement of Persephone. Hannah, by the elbow, urged
Persephone to stand, laughing, eyes joyous and cheering loudest
of all for Persephone.

"Persephone," said Judge Molloy, "we're so glad you've
chosen Stansfield as your new home."

Many around them rose again, as welcome by them to
Persephone. She bowed, smiling and sat. Was then her smile
vanished fast, seeing at stance, in doorway at the bottom of the
stage- yes it was!

Apollo- she stared, her eyes frozen across the hall to him. And on Apollo's face, a look she could not figure- a smile of kinds, pleased to find her, but in his eyes something she thought she'd never seen. She returned the smile from across and looked away.

The assembly went on, the sun pushing great light through the windows and across the Hall. In it, Persephone kept a hidden eye on Apollo. Apollo's gaze never left her, and until he was there he did not notice the Sheriff upon him.

CHAPTER 34
PLANTING

The tree, a sapling still, was planted in the field behind Academy Hall, with the class and families in full there to witness.

Eyes stayed delighted with Persephone but many drew then to this other stranger, then on the outskirts with Sheriff Cicero beside him.

Apollo stood tall among the mortals, the sun bright upon him. Even without his arrows and armor, barefoot and in a t-shirt and shorts, it was clear Apollo was of superior stature, over even the Sheriff.

"Who is that?"

Jessi looked over the crowd and saw him- standing wide-shouldered beside Evan's dad.

"I have no idea," she told Regina. Not long after, Evan and Cam arrived.

"You guys coming," Evan asked, "The Dash? Try and get a seat at the finish line," he winked at Regina, "where I can see you."

"We're coming," answered Regina.

"Hi Jess," Evan said leaning into her, his hands on her shoulders from behind for a moment before he and Cam left them. Jessi's stomach felt sick from it as they followed the others toward the track.

"Your shoes, son," said Cicero, looking down at Apollo's bare feet, "where are they?"

"Elsewhere," said Apollo looking down at the Sheriff.

"Okay, friend," Cicero said, his hand at his belt, "no more games. Let's see some ID."

"Please, please I know him" called out Persephone, coming there with Hannah just behind.

"Both of you," warned Cicero, "get yourselves someplace else- now! This is business of the Sheriff's Department."

The Sheriff moved fast for his club- reaching it, but by the time he'd grabbed for Apollo's wrist, the warrior'd shot for the Sheriff's club arm. With grip on Cicero's forearm, Apollo turned his broad back into the Sheriff's chest and with another turn slammed Cicero to the ground.

"No!"

Persephone yelled out and Apollo forgot the Sheriff. The goddess started toward him, her look to him pleading. Evan too yelled out, to his father, running to him, but a swarm of deputies and nearby men got to Cicero first. Persephone's look, still pleading to him, told Apollo clear. As they raised him and held him, Apollo, amidst the men upon him, saw the beg of Persephone's eyes and with the might of the mob combined was taken down. Cicero, recovered, cleared through them with a knee sharp to Apollo's ribs and his club pulled tight to Apollo's throat.

"Hey," shouted Hannah, but it was lost in the sudden confusion. Apollo, handcuffed, was led by Cicero away from the planting field. Deputies urged onlookers back to the assembly but attention first went to the road beyond the campus where an ambulance raced past.

Molly was there then too, reaching Hannah and Persephone before the girls could say a word more.

"Persephone," asked Molloy "is that someone you know?"

CHAPTER 35
WAKING

Hermes blinked, then jumped alive, still inside the van, the ladder beside him and beside it the young man. Quick, he felt and brought to his eyes the noose, still wrapped round his hand. It tugged gently.

Hermes was fast to Hannah's bedroom where the father lay still on the floor.

Hermes drew forward his hood, bowing low at the father's body and laying his hands gently over the man's eyes, closing them. Hermes then pressed his hand to the man's chest.

With a great gasp and more gasps after it, the father came alive- and with coughing breath scattering from him, in the air itself, Hermes made his fastest exit.

Hermes let the noose lead him again, outside. In the bed of a full bush beside the home, Hermes found buried Apollo's quiver. He thought fast of shouldering it, but heard sirens ringing out. Coming his way, Hermes knew, and footed off without Apollo's Silver.

His head raised and senses keen, Hermes tread the way the rope led, feeling sense too for flesh to take. The wailing sirens having passed him, Hermes reached the sign marking the turn into the Academy, coming upon a cat, panting in high grass of the road- bleeding from a vicious wound on its side, dying.

From where he hid, away from eyes, near the spotted, green-eyed feline fighting valiant but fast losing, Hermes gave look the way of the campus. Quiet where he was, save the labored wheeze of the cat, Hermes too could hear the festivity ahead.

He took the noose from his hand and placed it around his own neck.

Hooded, he knelt and took the cat's soul- its gray spots turning stark white, it sprang from the ground with vigor and was off- wearing round its neck the knotted rope, up the road, leaving not sign of Hermes behind.

CHAPTER 36
SHERIFF OF STANSFIELD

"We met in our travels," Persephone told Molloy. "He's come quite far," but Persephone did not press on after Apollo, being dragged off by Sheriff Cicero.

Inside Persephone great fear rose. She imagined at any moment Apollo would strike, her pleading look the only hope she had. If his heart to me is at all true, Persephone thought, my eyes will have reached him. She trembled with it- both the terror and fantastic elation at seeing him, the Champion of the Sun, having followed her through time to this bewildering place. Eric, seeing the girl troubled, put his arm around Persephone.

"I must go with him," Persephone said, turning gently away from Molloy.

"I'll come with you."

"No," said Persephone.

"Dad, no," said Hannah. "I'll go with Persephone. You can't leave," she said, arm out over the many people assembled on the Great Lawn. "They need you here."

Hannah kissed her father and was off, she and Persephone catching up with Cicero- his head leaned into his cruiser's backseat where Apollo sat.

"You're gonna tell me your name, son," Cicero gritted.

Coming quick through the parked cars in the lot was Dr. Miraz.

"Sheriff," he called out, saying no more once he saw Hannah and Persephone heading toward Cicero as well. "Sheriff, please tell me what you're doing with this young man? What is this?"

"This, Doctor," said Cicero, his eyes wild at Apollo, "is a wiseass punk who better tell me his goddamn name."

"Do you really want to create more of a scene? Here, today?"

"No," said Cicero, "I don't. So pretty boy can decide if he's gonna speak while we ride to the station."

Cicero slammed the car door shut and rounded for the driver's side.

"I'm coming," said Persephone, bringing halt to Cicero.

"Oh, now wait a minute," said Cicero. "Is that it? This another, what is it?- Norwegian? Another illegal?"

"Persephone is legal, Sheriff," said Hannah. "My father and I saw to it."

"I don't think this is any of your business, young lady- or your father's for that matter, and as for you," Cicero said pointing to Persephone, "You wanna come along? Get on in, 'cause frankly, I think…"

"I think it's best to discuss this at the station," said Miraz, stepping in.

"We'll sit in the back," said Hannah.

"The hell you will," said Cicero. "That young man is my prisoner!" The scent was faint but found Hannah then. She did not answer the Sheriff, his breath foul from liquor.

"Sheriff," said Dr. Miraz, "give me just a minute with Miss Molloy." Cicero stood, silent at his car door as Hannah stepped just away with the doctor.

"Maybe its best you stay here with you father, Hannah."

"No," said Hannah, "I'm going with Persephone."

"Hannah," said the doctor to her, leaning closer, "You-you don't want to-. Sheriff Cicero, you know."

"I'm going," Hannah said, starting past Miraz.

"Hannah, wait," said Miraz, stopping her," It's your father."

"What about my father?"

"You're not a child anymore, Hannah, and with your mother-, well, you just need to know this." Dr. Miraz pulled from his pocket a small pill bottle, handing it to Hannah. "Those are for your father. You see his name, there?" Hannah looked at the bottle, nodding, eyes soft at reading his name on it.

"Those are for his heart," said Miraz, "and he's to start them right away."

The shock hit Hannah fast, a numbness overcoming her; she thought she might faint away.

"Tell you what," said Miraz. "I'll go to the station, make sure your friends are okay. You take those to your dad. You know your father, he won't take them. It was all I could do to get him to let me write the script. Tell him, two of those tonight before bed, then just the one each night."

Hannah stood, still blank, holding the bottle.

"Hannah," said Miraz, "I'll go with Persephone. If there's any trouble, I'll phone."

"Yes," said Persephone, coming up behind them, "I agree with the doctor. Your place is here. I'll see to things with the Sheriff."

Hannah put the pills in her backpack and left to find her father, with Apollo riding off in Cicero's cruiser and Persephone off with Miraz behind them.

After all that had happened- all that had her so desperately low and fantastically high, all seemed small to Hannah suddenly. At her father's side, his pills in her pack, she felt suddenly a need to be close to him, and a sudden grief all over for what she nearly did in trying to take her own life. Sure she was, she'd have taken his too.

CHAPTER 37
THE STATION

Apollo was led and then imprisoned inside the Sheriff's station, knowing well what Persephone's look to him meant. Still, within him was the urge to break free and lay waste to the man called Cicero. The Sheriff tried to handle Apollo roughly, twisting his bound wrists and slamming his chest to the cell wall, vowing on some name unknown to make Apollo speak.

"If you really want to help your friend," said Miraz to Persephone, "you'll just tell us who he is- and who you are." Persephone knew not how to answer. "You've managed to fool a lot of people, but I don't fool so easy. Judge Molloy has wealth, influence- you've already benefitted, haven't you, Miss Hayes? - or whoever you are."

Persephone could not speak, in disbelief of the sudden darkness of the doctor.

"You've managed yourself a year of schooling and, apparently, board at their estate, but that was before your friend here arrived." Footsteps quieted Miraz. Cicero entered.

"Who is he," Cicero shot at Persephone. "I ain't kiddin', honey. Call just came through about trouble at the Molloys. Ted Becker was working there and apparently someone in the house surprised him. Someone else reported seeing your big, blonde friend- running from that direction toward campus! Breaking, entering, assault- so I'm telling you for the last time, your mute friend is gonna rot back there until I know more- you better talk, now!"

Persephone panicked, unable to speak. Cicero marched toward her.

"He your boyfriend, huh? You two a couple of thieves, run off? – get hitched without daddy's permission, that it?" Cicero asked, leaning in close on Persephone. "What is it," he said nearly in a whisper, his breath hot in her ear. From corner glance, Persephone caught sight of Miraz, coming closer too, from behind. Cicero's arms went for Persephone's shoulders but she spun away.

"Now, hold on," Cicero said, a smile spread across his face.

Persephone backed for the station door, but Miraz reached there first. He laid his hand on her spine.

"We can help you," Miraz told her, "your friend too. Stansfield's a nice, quiet place, Persephone. We can all get along nicely."

Dear Hannah, Persephone thought, for what happens I beg you forgive me.

CHAPTER 38
SWIM

Hannah had then seen the assembly end, sitting beside her father on the Great Lawn as the sun started its afternoon descent.

"We'll get to the Sheriff's station," Molloy told Hannah as they walked toward Eric's car, but suddenly, Hannah thought of her mother. The sun still coming down, Hannah thought of what her mother might make of things, real and unreal she'd seen. Of Persephone and Apollo, Hannah could not guess what Amy Molloy would think, but whether she believed them Gods or not, Hannah decided, Mom would welcome them. Of Hannah herself, and her fool act from the tree, her mother would be so upset- but forgiving, the girl was sure, and of Eric- she would think only to care for him.

"No," she said, "you know what? Persephone's there, so is Dr. Miraz. Why don't you just go home?"

"And you?"

"I think I'm gonna swim a few laps, clear my head. You go home- rest."

"I'll wait," said Eric.

"I'll walk," Hannah said, kissing his cheek and hugging goodbye. "Call me if you hear from Dr. Miraz. I'll come home for a shower and head to the station then if we haven't heard anything."

Eric smiled, wide with pride at her.

"You are so your mother."

So my mother, Hannah thought, the campus clearing out and sun nearly down as she head for the pool. Cool and feeling alive, Hannah broke the water and was under it- alone in the swimming pool. She spun herself and raised her head, then tread to the pool's wall where she stretched and straightened her cap. Energy unexplained ran through Hannah. The laps, she thought, would help burn some if it off. Was her nerves, she thought, and desperately she wanted to rest herself.

Her mother hardly slept, remembered Hannah, and managed to get so much done- always doing, planning, leading, fighting, running herself to the ground- for her family, and this town.

Hannah had not timed herself, but swam and felt as if at her fastest.

Stansfield- this town, Hannah thought. It took her mother from her in a way, Hannah believed, and thought again how it had nearly taken her too. Her next lap again felt fast, her legs their lightest and she decided to swim one more.

I won't be beaten by it, thought Hannah, not this town, not anyone or anything.

She reached the end of the lane and stretched her head up out of the water, taking a long breath- but at once, her eyes not yet clear, was driven back under.

CHAPTER 39
CAT'S EYES

A streak of white went past Persephone and Cicero screamed out.

Fast, it sprang off him and at Persephone's feet, hissing back at Miraz- the battle-torn white cat.

"Mother fucker," Cicero cursed, dabbing the blood from his cheek where the cat had clawed him. The cat leapt, and in a bounce was at the doctor's thigh, twisting up, claws cutting deep, and with teeth broke the flesh of Miraz. The doctor grabbed his buttocks, bellowing out and kicking at the cat, following the feline back toward the holding cells.

Cicero, with the back of his hand, wiped again at the blood, rolling fast from his face- three sharp lines across it where the freak cat slashed. Turning to Persephone he latched at her wrist, faster than she could find the door.

"Someone's gonna pay for that," he spat, his tongue licking where blood ran past his mouth.

Beyond them, Miraz turned towards the cat, arms out and at ready to corner it. Apollo, locked behind Miraz, eyed the cat- and the rope round its neck.

"C'mon, you little bitch," Miraz dared the cat, when at once he was reached- arm of Apollo outstretched snatched him fast and pulled him hard to the steel bars. The doctor's head landed with a sharp ring and he fell heavy to the floor.

"What the fuck was that," shouted Cicero from the front.

The cat padded softly then onto Miraz' chest, standing atop it.

Cicero approached and Apollo had no time to remain imprisoned. Seeing the rope round the cat, he knew at once that Hermes was there, and that Persephone was now in danger. Miraz's eyes fluttered open as Cicero reached them.

"Jesus," Cicero said, his face turned away. "What the fuck?"

Foggy, Miraz raised his head and saw the cat, looking him still in the eye. His brows, weak, went up and then fell. Away, still lying, Miraz fainted.

"Miraz," the Sheriff shouted, leaning down to him, but Cicero turned fast at hearing the loud metallic snap. Gun drawn and squared on his feet, Cicero had no time to wonder how Apollo stood before him, free.

CHAPTER 40
SHADOWS

She felt the force let off her head and Hannah shot up from the pool. At once she heard the laughter and knew it was Cam Landrum's, but closer to her was the hand that had pressed her down, now out, as if to help her.

"Hey, Hannah, give you a hand?"

Breathing fast, she stroked back, away from the pool wall, glaring at him- Evan Cicero.

"Suit yourself," said Evan. "Stay wet."

Hannah could not answer or even look his way then, backstroking with her eyes on the lights above the swim lanes.

"I just don't get why you can't be cool," Evan said. "After all, Hannah- nothing really happened, remember?"

"Please," Hannah said, feeling her lip begin to quiver. "Leave."

"Are you really gonna cry? Cam, she's gonna cry."

"Just, please," was all she could get out, her shaking then so great she could not say more.

"I can be here, you know," said Evan. "I can go anywhere I please. This is a small town and you and I both live here. Chances are we're gonna run into each other from time to time, so why don't you do everyone some good- either stay in your room with your fucking flute, or get over it. If anyone should be mad, it's me. You nearly ruined my name around here, but just remember Hannah- I could ruin yours just as fast."

Evan's cellphone chimed at Regina's call, and following its ring Regina was soon at the pool, Jessi with her.

"Evan," she said, her eyes like gouging hands at the sight of him with Hannah.

Evan turned. "I was just asking Hannah to thank her dad- Judge Molloy- the grant. You'll do that for me, won't you, Hannah?"

"Outside, Evan," said Regina, "now," and left, Jessi following. With satisfied smiles, Cam and Evan left too.

Out of the pool, Hannah dried herself, hearing no voices except the ones in her head. She slipped shorts and a tank top on and shouldered her pack, taking soft steps back toward the Great Lawn and home. Darkened by night, Regina and Jessi watched her.

"Let's follow her," said Regina.

"Let's not," said Jessi.

"What the hell's wrong with you? I told Evan I just wanted a chill night with you and you're acting like a huge loser!"

"Is this a chill night, following this fucking girl and throwing rocks at her?" Jessi stood from where they ducked in shadows and stepped out onto the path.

"Where are you going, Jessi?"

"Home, somewhere. I don't know," she said, heading alone for the campus gates. Just past them, a hand pressed first over her mouth and with a rustle of bushes and a smothered scream, Jessi was taken into the night.

CHAPTER 41
GUN DRAWN

Persephone entered, and still Cicero stood pointed at Apollo. His eyes shifted then, wary of them both.

"You get yourself right back into that pen, son. Don't you try me!"

Apollo's eyes locked on Cicero, on the barrel of the pistol pointed at him but then his eyes were drawn down where the white cat was at once on its paws atop the doctor. The cat turned its head to Persephone. She saw its black eyes gleam just before the cat turned back away and pounced off the doctor's chest for the door.

Apollo dove after it, missing, and was suddenly on the ground, his ears at alarm with deafening ring and a fierce burning at his shoulder

Persephone screamed just as his ears had blown and now her eyes locked wide on Apollo's. He could see her speaking but Apollo could hear not a word.

"He- he came at me! Goddamn it, why'd you do that?" Cicero's attention then turned fast to Persephone. "And don't you move either," Cicero said, taking aim with his pistol at Persephone. She held.

Apollo's senses started to return and he slid- his blood trailing in follow as it flow from his shoulder, back against the wall.

Cicero radioed then for the rest of his men.

CHAPTER 42
INCIDENT

The walk from the Academy to her home always reminded Hannah of her mother, bittersweet Stansfield would always carry her memory. At once, Hannah wanted her father's words to be true- that she was just as her mother was, as strong and bright and beloved.

Hannah rounded Academy Path and through Cobb field, a shortcut Amy taught her years before. Hannah ran then, seeing the yellow tape cordoning off the side of the house. Fast, she reached her father- in the driveway with a deputy's cruiser easing out past him.

"Dad, what is it?" Inside, Eric told her.

"Honey, there was- there was an incident here today while we were out. Your bedroom window- I had Ted Becker out to fix it. He was here today with his son, Teddy."

"I know Teddy," said Hannah.

"Well, Mr. Becker- he, he had a heart attack upstairs Hannah."

"Oh no," Hannah gasped.

"I know," said Eric," it's awful. They found him on the floor. Both of them- they're at the hospital now. I was thinking I'd go there."

"Dad, hang on," Hannah said. "Let's sit. We need to talk."

"That's a good idea," Eric said, pulling a chair for her. "I'm afraid there's a bit more to what happened here today."

They sat and Eric told Hannah that the deputy had waited there for him- to report to Judge Molloy the emergency call to his home and to advise that an investigation was pending- that Mr. Becker's heart attack may have come from great shock- of finding an intruder in the house, that it seemed as though nothing was missing.

"Teddy though," said Eric, "was knocked off a ladder, unconscious."

"Oh no," said Hannah.

"Yes, and his clothes were stolen from him- a t-shirt and cargo shorts. Hannah honey, wasn't Persephone's friend wearing cargo shorts?"

"Yes," Hannah said, disappointment spread across her face. "Did you hear from Dr. Miraz?"

"No," said Eric, "but I think we better go see on Persephone at the station, huh?"

Hannah's mind clouded quick from it all, but then she looked close at her father, strong with such weight on him but suddenly looking tired. The clouds of her thoughts broke as she reached for her pack.

"Dad, wait. Dr. Miraz, he gave me these for you."

Molloy's head hung at seeing the pills. Taking them from her he could not look his daughter in the eye.

"Dad," she said taking his hand, "I've been doing a lot of thinking, about everything- about Mom. You always take care of me but I need to take care of you too, like Mom would."

Molloy nodded, pride lifting his heart and eyes to her.

"I'll go to the station, alone. I'll call you from there."

"Hannah, no…"

"Daddy, yes- you let Persephone into our home, our lives- we both did, but- but this is on me, ok? I'll handle this one- and no hospital for you tonight either. I think you've had enough for one day."

Hannah felt good and Molloy did not challenge her. She showered and changed and on her way out of her bedroom flicked off her light. It was then she saw it, beneath her bed- the stone's faded glow.

As she pulled in to the station, she saw the lot was jammed with what looked like Stansfield's full forces- every cruiser, a pair of motorcycles and two department vans, all parked in slant at the station doors. Entering past it all, she saw first Dr. Miraz.

"Your friend," said Miraz to Hannah, holding a compress to his skull, "and that friend of hers- there's nothing you can do for them now."

"Where are they?"

"Being held, both of them. Do you and your dad a favor, Hannah. Turn around and go home."

She made her way through the mob of uniforms, direct to Sheriff Cicero.

"I'd like to see them."

"Forget it," said Cicero.

"It's my right," said Hannah, "and Persephone's."

"If that's even her name, " said Cicero.

"I'm doing you the courtesy of speaking softly, Sheriff Cicero," she said, "but if you want to discuss the law with me, I'm going to make sure every deputy in this room hears how a sixteen year old girl completely embarrasses you on the subject."

Cicero, face bandaged with blood seeping muted red through, fought an urge to strike something. Hannah saw his eyes, as if bleeding too.

"They're around the corner in holding," he told Hannah. "You got five minutes."

CHAPTER 43
WOUNDED

"Listen well, Apollo. This realm of Earth, we are in another place, truest. We are suns forward, Apollo- do you see? Our forces are not as in Olympus."

It was the first moment Persephone could speak, though softly, to Apollo, with armed deputies standing near as Apollo lay, wounded and bound to a wheeled gurney. Even then, as Apollo hissed through his teeth at the pain of his wound, Persephone was not sure he understood.

"Tales of Olympus are written here," she said. "I've seen them- and how greatly the scribes through time have deceived."

It was all Persephone could say before the medics, flanked by deputies, pulled Apollo away from her, still shackled.

Hannah passed Apollo, at once with horror. Persephone called to her and Hannah went to her embrace.

"What's happening?"

"This is what's happening," said Cicero entering, coming straight at Persephone and taking her wrist.

"Hey," yelled Hannah, but Cicero carried on- handcuffing Persephone to the wall, behind a bench the Sheriff shoved her down on. "Hey," Hannah yelled louder.

"Aiding and abetting," said Cicero, "B&E, assault!"

"Assault?"

"Pretty boy banged up the doctor, took a run at me, and in case he's still feeling frisky at the hospital, Miss Hayes is staying right here. He was trying to rob your father, Hannah. Someone saw him fleeing the scene. Those are Teddy Becker's clothes he's got on! Maybe your friend can tell you what he was doing inside your house? "

Hannah and Persephone looked at each other, silent amid the shuffling activity in and outside the station.

"Four minutes," Cicero said, leaving past deputies still stationed at the door.

More deputies accompanied the medics carrying Apollo. Miraz rode along with one, as a precaution, he told Cicero. True he was shaken, but thought wiser to stay near this one he heard called Apollo. Hannah remained at the station.

"Why," asked Hannah low. "Why are you allowing this?"

"What should I do," Persephone asked back. "The Sheriff, his men…"

"You're a goddess," said Hannah, "with powers. I've seen them!"

"You've seen your own," Persephone told her. "The lightning- that morning in your room, after your window was broken."

Hannah, eyes full, nodded.

"Was not my lightning, Hannah. Was yours."

Hannah, eyes wide did not speak. Cicero entered again to tell her that time was up. Hannah rose and hugged Persephone.

"I'll get you out of here."

Outside in front of the station, the buzz of before had died down. At the bottom of the station steps Hannah tried, and again at the car she tried to reach her father on the phone, but Eric Molloy did not answer.

Looking up, Hannah saw the star-filled night sky, and asked the heavens all to help her. The sky answered, or so it seemed to Hannah, with a racing across of stone gray clouds, like fast-moving fog high overhead.

Soon after, soft rain began to fall. Hannah, quick as the clouds, head for home.

CHAPTER 44
BOUND

Miraz would be okay. His bell had been rung, a concussion, but sensed no other real damage.

Apollo though still bled- and his eyes, blazing gold, shifted from face to face in survey of the scene. Around him these men gathered, with attention to his wound and beyond them more men, in uniform near the doorway. He did not see Persephone, Hermes or the one called Cicero. He could hear none but the steady ring, high-pitched pressing in his skull.

At once another arrived, bringing news to those at the door, saying something that sent all but two armed men off. Those tending his wound seemed to stir. Miraz rose. Apollo surveyed all.

They had shackled him down, at the ankles and wrists, and strapped him down at the chest. Apollo wondered then if he would ever see Olympus- see her again. Persephone, he thought, I must find Persephone.

Miraz spoke to those nearest Apollo, urging them away and took over the care of Apollo's wound. With caution he was at Apollo's side, assuring the two on guard at the door that all was fine. Still Apollo could not hear, but on the doctor's face was a look he knew was meant for him. As Persephone, still imprinted in Apollo, had begged him not to bring rise- the only reason he'd not yet broken free and gone berserk, Miraz too seemed to plead in a way, his eyes a glow their own.

Miraz pressed his hand to Apollo's chest, as if to calm him, his mouth moving and his eyes to the doorway.

Apollo swallowed deep and the pressing in his ears relented slightly, the doctor's voice a low wordless hum. Apollo swallowed once more.

"...Persephone," Miraz said softly, glancing down at Apollo. "Cicero's holding her. The two of you are in pretty deep. If you follow me," he whispered, " I can help get you out of it. I want to know though- who are you, and why are you in Stansfield?"

The two at the door were far enough. With his eyes, Apollo beckoned Miraz closer.

"My name is Apollo," he told him low, "and I am here for the one you tell of- the goddess Persephone."

"Goddess?"

"Yes," said Apollo, "of all the sky, of life true- and this place Stansfield I will crush if need be to return her."

Miraz kept his eyes darting from Apollo to the door.

"If you bring me to her," Apollo told him, "I will spare you."

Sideways Miraz glanced again, toward the deputies at the door, and then back down to Apollo.

"I can," Miraz said nodding, "I can bring you to her."

"Your name."

"Miraz," he said, "Dr. Miraz."

"Know this, Miraz," said Apollo, "if you cross me, your end will be most cruel."

Before Miraz could ponder it, Apollo lunged and seized his throat, snapping free his wrists and clutching with the arm closest to the doctor. Miraz' head pounded fast, about to burst it felt and yet again the doctor faded unconscious.

From the doorway they came fast, weapons drawn, clicking footsteps and arms.

"Don't move!"

"Let go of the doctor!"

His legs bound low together, Apollo lifted them free and over his head he rolled them- his shackles crashing into the approaching guards. Still holding Miraz he then heaved his chest free and rose to his feet.

The deputies felled, Apollo eyed their weapons and with his free hand snatched one off the ground. Before either man could get back his wind, Apollo had slung Miraz over his shoulder and with gun in hand was gone with him.

CHAPTER 45
DEATHBED

Molloy would not answer. Beside his bed was the bottle she'd handed him just hours before. As she called out to him, each time louder, thunder too growled louder outside. As she shook him, it rumbled heavy behind the clouds and when Hannah imagined the very worst she let out a scream. Lightning, like cannon fire, echoed over the steady rain.

She trembled, backing toward the door and then screamed again, turning, already in tears, to see who or what blocked her.

There in Molloy's bedroom he stood silent, his chin chalk white all Hannah could see of his face beneath the hood.

Hannah fell, distant-eyed and weeping, as if elsewhere herself as Hermes eased past her. He went to her father's side and spoke. His voice confused her in its cool and easy tone. A boy's voice, she thought, so surprised by it that his words did not register.

"Can you," Hermes asked, "can you- see me?"

Her sobs silent, she started again to shake. Hannah turned, rising.

"Who the hell are you?"

Hermes, hood hanged over her father's bed, stood silent again.

"I don't care- who, or what you are," Hannah said standing, "you get the hell away from my father!"

Thunder rolled deep beneath her snarl and still silent, Hermes slowly stepped back from the bed. He'd heard it, looking to the rattling window from it, then turned his head to Hannah.

"Who are you," she asked, searching for his face, "a god- or are you Death?"

Her lips trembled. Her words seemed to fight their way from her mouth between the chattering of her gritted teeth as she asked.

"What do you want?"

The sky seemed to shake above them, the air of the room feeling thick and charged. Hannah felt it in herself- electric.

"Answer me," Hannah shouted, and a crackle sliced through the night, filling it fast bright white before striking down somewhere near. Hannah's eyes smoldered dark in that moment, deep shadows cutting her skin in that flash of lightning that illuminated the room. Slow, Hermes pulled back his hood.

"I want- to help you."

And the face of a boy, Hannah thought, as he turned, his cheekbones high and full- colorless soft flesh. Hermes bent, his hood falling forward as he leaned over Molloy, lifeless in his bed. From behind the hood, Hannah saw a glow- a breath of light blue fill the air like a halo round them both, and in another breath it was gone. Hermes raised his head and turned back toward her.

"Who are you," she asked him again as the rain fell softer but steady in the quiet.

He seemed to want to speak, his eyes large at hers, and seemed to nearly start, but then did not. Hermes saw in her something reminding him of Persephone, and fast an affinity grew- but immense over it was his bewilderment.

Hannah's eyes still searched him, for some hint of something to at least settle her trembling, but in their directness her eyes gave not a hint of her fear.

"That," said Hannah pointing to her chin, "around your neck."

His hand went to it, the knotted rope. Her eyes moved closer to it with a step forward.

"Where'd you get that?"

Again, Hermes seemed about to speak, but then he breathed deep and before Hannah could ask more was gone.

Hannah too breathed deep and rushed to her father. Her head tilted, she saw his chest fall and rise.

"Daddy," she said soft-throated, patting him, "Daddy, wake up."

"Hannah," he answered, his eyes closed still.

"Daddy, you-," she began, "I thought you – are you alright?"

"Yes, honey," he told her, eyes slivers and falling.

She sat at his side, her hand then in his, looking out the window to the rain. Fixing it in her mind, the rain fell harder and then relented again as her thought let go.

Molloy was that fast asleep again. Hannah with close eye saw her father breathing easy and she let her attention return to the rain. In her mind she envisioned it and her design was then drawn in the sky. From the window she watched, the stars- like lighthouses in the ocean of night, beacons in the haze of clouds, and as if guiding it to harbor Hannah led it, just as she dreamt it, with power and force from the sky- thunder, that grew and grew from somewhere in the black like a wave. It stirred Molloy from his sleep. Her hand still in his, he tightened his grip.

"Hannah," he said, his eyes still not open.

"It's me, Daddy," Hannah said, "It's me. Go back to sleep."

Molloy's grip loosened and Hannah rose to let him sleep, stepping quiet out of the room, down the stairs and out into the rain. From the front door Hannah started and walked down to the lawn, the clouds parting and drying her path. The moon loomed large above in the absence of the rainclouds, sending Hannah's blood to race. She raised her head to it and painted it in her mind, and born from that same brushstroke, in the distance, a twinkling bright blaze cut through the gray-shining, falling fast like a race of stars- lightning.

Hannah closed her eyes and willed it, as if forcing it from the moon, and growing then over the beating of her heart, over the beating of the rain against the ground on either side of her, Hannah heard it- the roll and sudden clap of thunder.

II. A TALE TOLD NETHER

"Hear the tale just told to me- of Apollo, North of Nether- by a mortal slain!"

"Slain?- You say Apollo is slain!?"

"North of Nether," shouted another. "Is there no sun for mighty Apollo to feast from?"

"That place has sun," said the first, "a sun most cursed, and beneath it lays more- left there is fair, Persephone!"

Listeners shrieked and ran to tell others. Theories were born from each word of it as it spread- from the River- further and further as if spider's web, from mouth of one to ears of many- spinning far from where the first had sat, on the fallen branch of the Dark Oak.

"Powerless to save Apollo, Persephone stays locked there- and Harvest's End looms!"

"This tale you were told," said another, "then tell by who!"

"Yes," agreed another," Who tells you of Apollo's Fall?"

"Yes, say who!"

"I cannot," said the first.

"Bah, tales! Great Zeus himself would crush all North of Olympus if it were true!"

By some it was dismissed then and never left that place at Styx, but for others the tale was too fantastic not to tell, and so it went, the terror greater and greater with each telling, that tale told at the Dark Oak. Further it reached, rendered rough in its travels, to directions all, until as whispers on the last of summer's breezes it was carried to Olympus, the Tale of the Fall of Apollo, of the taking of Persephone, and as it carried on and on, both North and South of there it was spoken, that Harvest's End with the Goddess Persephone not returned would leave all starved and desperate, leave the land ravaged and the sea wild, leave all to arms and savagery and leave all Olympus- Ever Cold.

Enjoy the book? Are you ready for the next installment of the series? Please help us to spread the word about Hannah and the Gods of Olympus by **liking us on Facebook** and telling your friends about the book. Let them borrow it for free if you like. We don't mind you sharing. ☺

It is VERY IMPORTANT to stay connected. Let's make this a series that no one will ever forget! We look forward to your feedback and your comments online!

Also please be sure to visit us online with any of the links listed below.

www.facebook.com/godsofolympusbooks
www.theGodsofOlympus.com
www.MaidenComics.com